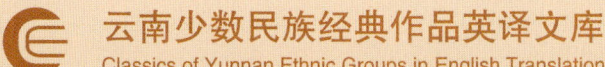

云南少数民族经典作品英译文库

Classics of Yunnan Ethnic Groups in English Translation

主编 李昌银　General Editor　Li Changyin

副主编 黄瑛 彭庆华　Associate General Editors　Huang Ying & Peng Qinghua

Pamichali

帕米查哩

演唱◎尔千次里　熊巴光布

熊巴温独　熊巴将楚等

汉译◎汤格·萨甲博

记录整理◎李理

英译◎刘德周

译校◎[美]包琼

Sung by Erqian Cili et al

Translated from Pumi into Chinese by Tangge Sajiabo

Recorded & Edited by Li Li

Translated from Chinese into English by Liu Dezhou

Revised by Joan Cecile Boulerice

云南出版集团

云南人民出版社

图书在版编目（CIP）数据

　帕米查哩：汉、英 / 尔千次里等演唱；汤格·萨
甲博汉译；李理记录整理；刘德周英译. -- 昆明：云
南人民出版社，2018.12
　（云南少数民族经典作品英译文库 / 李昌银主编）
　ISBN 978-7-222-17503-7

　Ⅰ.①帕… Ⅱ.①尔… ②汤… ③李… ④刘… Ⅲ.
①普米族—叙事诗—中国—汉、英 Ⅳ.①I222.7
　中国版本图书馆CIP数据核字(2018)第277433号

出 品 人　李　维　赵石定
项目统筹　周　祥　殷筱钊
项目组稿　郭木玉
责任编辑　郭木玉　任建红　李东华
设计制作　马　滨　三人禾
责任校对　卫佳睿　崔苡菡　付芳侠　周桉吉
责任印制　陆卫华　代隆参

云南少数民族经典作品英译文库
Classics of Yunnan Ethnic Groups in English Translation

帕米查哩
Pamichali

演唱◎尔千次里　熊巴光布　熊巴温独　熊巴将楚等
汉译◎汤格·萨甲博
记录整理◎李理
英译◎刘德周
译校◎[美]包琼

Sung by Erqian Cili et al
Translated from Pumi into Chinese by Tangge Sajiabo
Recorded & Edited by Li Li
Translated from Chinese into English by Liu Dezhou
Revised by Joan Cecile Boulerice

出　版　云南出版集团　云南人民出版社
发　行　云南人民出版社
社　址　昆明市环城西路609号
邮　编　650034
网　址　www.ynpph.com.cn
E-mail　ynrms@sina.com
开　本　787mm×1092mm　1/16
印　张　10.25
字　数　150千
版　次　2018年12月第1版第1次印刷
印　刷　云南出版印刷（集团）有限责任公司　云南新华印刷一厂
书　号　ISBN 978-7-222-17503-7
定　价　58.00元

云南人民出版社
公众微信号

序 一

◎李正栓

民族典籍英译是传播中国文化、文学和文明的重要途径，是中华文化走出去的重要组成部分。文化与文学的传播，是一个国家提高文化软实力的重要方式，在文化交流和文明建设中起着不可或缺的作用，对提高国家对外话语权、构建国家对外话语体系以及对建设世界文学都有积极意义。

中国各少数民族拥有许多优秀的典籍，具有很高的文物价值、文学价值和文化价值。各民族的先人们通过口头流传或用文字记述了他们各具特色的文化。各少数民族几乎都有自己民族的创世史、史诗和神话传说。

中国民族典籍独具特色，不可替代。重视民族典籍的翻译和研究工作，对于挖掘各民族优秀文化，保护各民族文明，增强各民族之间的沟通和了解，进一步向世界其他地区传播各少数民族优秀文化，乃至提高我国文化软实力都有着重要意义。不少少数民族聚居地处于祖国边疆，有的处在"一带一路"建设关键部位，有的处在与周边国家进行各种交流的重要位置。

中国民族典籍是世界多元文化的有机组成部分，与其他文化共同造就了世界文化的绚丽多姿。世界正因为其文化多样性才变得缤纷多彩。我国各民族典籍中包含的文化多样性极大地丰富了世界多元、特色鲜明的文化。人们对多样性形成全新的认识角度和思维方式。多样性开阔了人们的视野，丰富了人们思考问题的角度。挖掘这些典籍中所蕴含的教育价值和文化价值，对世界其他民族都有指导和借鉴意义，并且有助于建设我国的文化自信。

民族典籍本身蕴含的特殊价值对加强民族文化了解、促进中外文化交流具有重大意义。民族典籍英译具有文学翻译和文化传递之功能，有对外宣传作用，还是一种文学外交。因此，民族典籍翻译和研究对于维护祖国统一、促进民族团结、稳定边疆以及增强国内各民族和中外文化之间的交流都起着极为重要的作用。

中华人民共和国成立以后，中央政府一直十分重视民族典籍翻译和研究工作，提供了强有力的政策支持，并采取了一系列有效措施，加快了各少数民族典籍的抢救、整理、翻译和研究的进程。中央政府多次召开西藏工作会议和新疆工作会议。近年来，国际和国内对于多元文化高度关注，少数民族文学典籍的翻译已然成为业内研究的热点。

近年来，民族典籍翻译和研究迅猛发展，势头良好。国家大力支持，发放国家社科基金课题，教育部和国家民委也发放课题，扶持了一大批研究者。很多民族典籍翻译课题得以立项并顺利开展；为数不少的民族典籍被翻译成汉语、英语和其他语言并出版发行；越来越多的业界人士致力于这个满富生机的学术领域。

在中国文化走出去的国家战略下，全国少数民族典籍英译学术研讨会陆续召开，已经召开三次。

　　云南是中国民族最多的省份。人口在 5000 人以上的少数民族有 25 个，其中有 15 个民族为云南所特有，分别是：白族、哈尼族、傣族、傈僳族、佤族、拉祜族、纳西族、景颇族、布朗族、普米族、阿昌族、基诺族、怒族、德昂族、独龙族。其中除白族人口占全国白族人口总数的 84% 以上外，其他 14 个民族 95% 居住在云南。

　　云南还是我国跨境民族最多的省份。在云南的 25 个少数民族中，有 16 个民族跨境而居，分别是：傣族、壮族、苗族、景颇族、瑶族、哈尼族、德昂族、佤族、拉祜族、彝族、阿昌族、傈僳族、布依族、怒族、布朗族、独龙族。

　　云南少数民族创造了辉煌的文化。据不完全统计，云南少数民族文字文献古籍蕴藏量达 10 万余册（卷），口传古籍 4 万余种。云南省民委少数民族古籍整理出版规划办公室为了挽救和保护这些古籍，计划在 5 年内编纂出版 100 卷《云南少数民族古籍珍本集成》。这是一个令人瞩目的庞大计划。将这些古籍中的珍品翻译介绍给世界，不仅能够弘扬云南省丰富多彩的民族文化，而且有助于增进与南亚东南亚国家的理解与交流，为"一带一路"倡议的实施做出贡献。

　　云南师范大学外国语学院很重视这一领域的工作。在外国语学院领导支持下，李昌银教授带领一个由教授和中青年学者组成的团队对精选出来的 17 部云南少数民族经典作品进行英译，计划在 5 年内（"十三五"期间）翻译出版。这是一项十分有意义的宏大工程。

　　这 17 部民族典籍，内容全部为各民族的英雄史诗或神话传说，具有很高的历史意义和文学价值。这些作品涉及阿昌族、白族、傣族、德昂族、哈尼族、景颇族、拉祜族、苗族、纳西族、普米族、彝族等 11 个少数民族。

云南师范大学这支翻译队伍实力强大，主要由一些多年从事翻译教学、研究和实践的教授和副教授组成，他们是李昌银、黄瑛、彭庆华、孙兴文、吴相如、刘德周、杨慧芳、邰菊、陈萍、包琼（Joan Boulerice）等国内外专家学者。他们在云南翻译界都是风云人物。

在民族典籍英译中，这支队伍异军突起，为我国民族典籍英译壮大了声势，必将为中国民族典籍走向世界而成为世界文学的一部分做出新贡献。

民族典籍翻译与研究事业关乎国家的稳定统一，关乎民族关系的和谐发展，关乎世界多元文化的实现。在中国，民族典籍资源极为丰富，有待进一步挖掘、翻译。因此，民族典籍英译前景光明。同时，我们也应意识到，仍有许多濒临消失的少数民族典籍亟待拯救，民族典籍翻译与研究工作任重而道远。

（李正栓，中国英汉语比较研究会典籍英译专业委员会常务副会长兼秘书长）

Foreword by Li Zhengshuan

The translation of Chinese ethnic classics is an important approach in spreading Chinese culture, literature and civilization. It is a crucial component of Chinese culture going global. The spreading of Chinese culture and literature is a national policy and an important way to improve the cultural soft power of China. It plays an indispensable role in the cultural exchange between China and other countries and the development of world literature.

The ethnic groups in China have countless excellent classics with high anthropological, literary and cultural value. The ancestors of each ethnic group have passed down their distinctive culture orally or in writing. Almost all the ethnic groups have their own story of creation, epics, myths and legends.

Chinese ethnic classics are unique and irreplaceable. It is imperative to attach importance to the translation and research of ethnic classics; to explore the excellent ethnic cultures; to protect the civilization of ethnic groups; to enhance the communication and understanding among ethnic groups; to further spread the outstanding culture of ethnic groups to other parts of the world; and to build the cultural strength of China. Many ethnic groups live in the border areas and thus play an important role in the cultural and economic cooperation between China and its neighbors in the context of the Belt and Road Initiative.

Chinese ethnic classics are an important component of the magnificence and diversity of world culture. It is diversity that makes the world so colorful. The cultural diversity of Chinese ethnic classics has greatly enriched the world's pluralism and its distinctive features. People around the world have formed a new understanding of diversity. This diversity has expanded people's horizon and enriched their way of thinking. Digging out the educational and cultural value in these classics can contribute to the construction of China's self-confidence in culture.

The special value of the ethnic classics itself is of great significance to the strengthening of national culture and intercultural communication between China and foreign countries. The translation of ethnic classics is not just a literary exchange, but also a form of cultural communication. It is diplomacy through literature in that it consolidates the cultural ties between China and other countries.

After the founding of the People's Republic of China, the central government attached great importance to the translation and research of ethnic classics, provided the a great deal of policy support, and adopted a series of effective measures to speed up the process of rescuing, collating, translating and studying ethnic classics. The central government has convened several working conferences on Tibet and Xinjiang. In recent years, both China and other countries have paid close attention to multiculture. The translation of ethnic classics has become a hot topic.

In recent years, the translation and research of ethnic classics have progressed rapidly and have shown good prospects. The government strongly supports and grants the research projects of the national social science fund. The Ministry of Education and the State Ethnic Affairs Commission are also issuing research projects and giving funding to a large number of researchers. Many research projects on ethnic classics have been approved and carried out. Many ethnic classics have been translated into Chinese, English and other languages and published. More and more professionals have dedicated themselves to this new sphere of learning.

In this context, the academic conferences on translation of ethnic classics are held one after another all around the country. And up to now three have been held.

Yunnan is the province which has the most ethnic groups in China. Besides Han people, there are 25 ethnic groups, each with a population of more than 5,000. Among them, 15 ethnic groups are unique to Yunnan, which are the Bai, the Hani, the Dai, the Lisu, the Wa, the Lahu, the Naxi, the Jingpo, the Bulang, the Pumi, the Achang, the Jinuo, the Nu, the De'ang and the Dulong. Among these, 84% of the total number of the Bai people in China and 95% of the other 14 ethnic groups are living in Yunnan.

Yunnan is also the province which has the most cross-border ethnic groups. Of the 25 ethnic groups, 16 live across the border, namely: the Dai, the Zhuang, the Miao, the Jingpo, the Yao, the Hani, the De'ang, the Wa, the Lahu, the Yi, the Achang, the Lisu, the Buyi, the Nu, the Bulang and the Dulong.

The ethnic groups in Yunnan have created splendid cultures. According to statistics, the number of classics of Yunnan ethnic groups is more than 100 thousand volumes and classics in oral tradition are more than 40 thousand. In order to save and protect these ancient books, the Office of Classics Collation and Publishing of Yunnan Ethnic Groups Affairs Commission planned to compile and publish 100 volumes of *A Collection of Yunnan Ethnic Group Rare Books* in five years, which is an ambitious plan. The introduction of the ancient classics via translation can not only promote and develop the colorful ethnic cultures of Yunnan, but also contribute to the understanding and exchange between China and countries in South Asia and Southeast Asia and to the implementation of the Belt and Road Initiative as well.

The School of Foreign Languages and Literature of Yunnan Normal University is paying close attention to this field. With the support of the School and the University, Professor Li Changyin is leading a group of professors and young scholars to do the project of *"Classics of Yunnan Ethnic Groups in English Translation"*, which includes 17 ethnic classics selected carefully from Yunnan's bountiful ethnic classics. These books are the heroic epics or myths and legends of each ethnic groups with great historical significance and literary value. They will finish the translation in five years (during "the thirteenth five-year plan"). After that, all the works will be published by Yunnan People's Publishing House.

The 17 works cover 11 ethnic groups: the Achang, the Bai, the Dai, the De'ang, the Hani, the Jingpo, the Lahu, the Miao, the Naxi, the Pumi and the Yi. All of these groups except the Miao and the Yi are unique to Yunnan.

The translation team of Yunnan Normal University is full of strength and vitality, composed of professors and associate professors who have been occupied in translation teaching, research, and practice for a long time. They are Li Changyin, Huang Ying, Peng Qinghua, Sun Xingwen, Wu Xiangru, Liu Dezhou, Yang Huifang, Gao Ju, Chen Ping, Joan Boulerice and other experts and scholars who are representative figures in the translation field in Yunnan province.

This team is a new force that has suddenly arisen in terms of translating ethnic classics. It is expanding the momentum of ethnic classics translation in China and has made a new contribution for China's ethnic classics to go global and become a part of world literature.

The translation and research of ethnic classics are related

to the development of Chinese culture and the realization of multiculturalism in the world. In China, ethnic classics are extremely rich in resources, which require us to make further exploration and research and translate them into other languages. Therefore, the future of translating ethnic classics is bright. At the same time, we should also realize that there are still many ethnic works which are close to extinction and urgently need to be rescued. We still have a long way to go in the fields of translation and research in ethnic classics.

(Li Zhengshuan, Standing Vice Chairman and Secretary General, Classics Translation Committee of CACSEC)

序 二

◎王 宏

好友云南师范大学外国语学院李昌银教授来电嘱托我为"云南少数民族经典作品英译文库"的出版写一序言，并随即发来该文库的背景资料，让我"不着急，慢慢写"。我本人从事中国典籍英译及研究，深知少数民族典籍对外传译的重要性，但又是少数民族典籍翻译的门外汉。因此，我是怀着虚心学习的态度来写此序言的。近年来，在中国文化"走出去"战略工程大背景下，在中央和地方各级政府的大力支持下，我国少数民族典籍的对外传译及研究工作顺利开展，取得了很大的进步。请看以下数据：

2008年，广西百色学院韩家权教授获批国家社科基金项目《布洛陀史诗》（壮汉英对照）。该项目已顺利结项，并于2013年12月获得中国民间文艺最高奖"山花奖"。

2012年，广西百色学院外语系翻译团队翻译的国家级非物质文化遗产《壮族嘹歌》（英文版）由广西师范大学出版社正式出版。

2012年，东北大学秦皇岛分校吴松林教授主编的《蒙古族系列：江格尔（汉英对照）》（上下册）由吉林大学出版社出版。

2013年，河北师范大学李正栓教授英译《藏族格言诗》

由长春出版社出版发行。

2013 年，云南财经大学崔晓霞教授撰写的《〈阿诗玛〉英译研究》收入由王宏印教授主编、民族出版社出版的"民族典籍翻译研究丛书"。

2014 年，东北大学秦皇岛分校吴松林教授撰写的《满族档案文献研究》申请到国家社科后期资助，他英译的《英雄格斯尔可汗》由吉林大学出版社出版。

2014 年，中南民族大学张立玉教授主持的"土家族主要典籍英译及研究"获批国家社科基金项目。

2015 年，西安外国语大学梁真惠副教授撰写的《〈玛纳斯〉翻译传播研究》收入由王宏印教授主编、民族出版社出版的"民族典籍翻译研究丛书"。

与此同时，第一届和第二届全国少数民族典籍英译学术研讨会分别于 2012 年和 2014 年在广西民族大学和大连民族学院举行，参加会议的院校分布之广、与会代表数量之众、提交论文数量之多和涉及研究话题之细，十分可喜。2016 年还将在中南民族大学举行第三届全国少数民族典籍英译学术研讨会。

为什么少数民族典籍的对外传译及研究工作在短短几年就受到译界的青睐，取得众多成果？我认为，这在很大程度上归于典籍翻译界乃至翻译界同仁对"中国典籍"的重新思考和认识。中国典籍浩如烟海，卷帙浩繁，举世瞩目，是全人类共同的精神财富。但对于中国典籍的理解，我们以前较多限于汉民族的重要文献和书籍，而对少数民族多有忽略。在讨论中国典籍时，也较多关注古代文学作品。其实，中国典籍指"中国清代末年1911年以前的重要文献和书籍",这就要求我们从事典籍翻译时,不但要翻译古代文学典籍作品,还要翻译古代哲学、科技、法律、医学、经济、军事、天文、地理等诸多方面的典籍作品,不但要翻译汉民族的典籍作品,也要翻译各少数民族的典籍作品。

民族典籍具有该民族的原型符号的特质,蕴藏着能够"遗传"并不断"再生"的文化基因。民族典籍是中华传统文化的内核,同时还是中华传统文化的符号构成规则。中国是具有56个民族的多民族国家,少数民族典籍是我国少数民族勤劳与智慧的结晶,是中华文明、也是世界文明不可或缺的一部分。少数民族典籍对外传译具有跨文化交流的作用,它不但有助于更多的人了解少数民族的独特文化,而且还有助于保护少数民族文化的独特性、维持少数民族文化多样性、促进各民族团结、提升中华文化软实力等。

中国少数民族典籍涉及宗教、文学、历史、语言、医学、天文历算等领域,内容丰富,版本多样,载体特殊,传承奇特。仅以《中国少数民族古籍总目提要》为例,该书于1997年正式立项,全书总体设计约60卷、110册,目前已出版23个民族卷共20册:纳西族卷、白族卷、东乡族卷·裕固族卷·保安族卷、土族卷·撒拉族卷、锡伯族卷、哈尼族卷、回族卷·铭刻、柯尔克孜族卷、羌族卷、毛南族卷·京族卷、仫佬族卷、达斡尔族卷、土家族卷、鄂温克族卷、鄂伦春族卷、赫哲族卷、苗族卷、侗族卷、黎族卷、朝鲜族卷。该书真实地反映了我国各少数民族古籍赋存的全面情况,充实了中国的历史和文化内容,为后人探索各种文化形式的源流、揭示中国社会文化发展的轨迹提供了极为珍贵的资料，为我国乃至世界各国人文科学研究提供了一套新颖而全面的资料，对于弘扬中华民族传统文化具有深远的历史意义和现实意义。

少数民族典籍的对外传译是一项艰巨的工作，涉及将少数民族语言译成汉语、少数民族语言之间的互译和少数民族语言译成外语（主要是英语）。前两类翻译历史源远流长，最早可追溯到春秋战国时代《越人歌》的翻译，即汉、壮语之间的翻译。少数民族典籍译成外语的时间则要晚一些。据考证，维吾尔族古典长诗《福乐智慧》成书于 1069 年或 1070 年，目前尚未发现完整的原稿，只存留下来三个抄本，分别为赫拉特抄本、费尔干纳抄本与埃及抄本，其中费尔干纳抄本于 12~13 世纪用阿拉伯文纳斯赫体抄写，1914 年发现于今中亚乌孜别克斯坦纳曼干城，现存于该共和国科学院东方研究所。这是少数民族典籍译介到国外的最早纪录。少数民族典籍外译在现代有了较快发展。一些少数民族典籍，如藏族的《格萨尔王传》、蒙古族的《江格尔》和柯尔克孜族的《玛纳斯》等英雄史诗，云南彝族的《阿诗玛》、维吾尔族的《艾里甫和赛乃姆》等民间叙事长诗已先后被翻译成英语及其他外国文字，为世人所知。这对传承少数民族经典，推动中外文化交流起到了不可替代的作用。然而，还有大量的中国少数民族典籍等待我们去翻译和研究。

云南省少数民族典籍资源十分丰富。据不完全统计，云南少数民族文字文献古籍蕴藏量达 10 万余册（卷），口传古籍 4 万余种。"云南少数民族经典作品英译文库"正是依托云南省丰富的少数民族典籍资源，借助云南师范大学外国语学院强大的翻译师资队伍，在云南人民出版社的有力支持下，首次将云南少数民族经典作品成系列对外译介的大力举措。云南师范大学外国语学院对"云南少数民族经典作品英译文库"十分重视，他们首先邀请省内外少数民族语言文化研究专家对云南民族典籍和民族文化经典作品进行筛选，做到"好中选好，优中选优"，同时调配最强的翻译力量承担文库的翻译任务。我粗略看了该文库的选题，发现选题面广，覆盖范围宽，收入了云南省阿昌族、白族、傣族、纳西族、德昂族、哈尼族、景颇族、拉祜族、苗族、普米族和彝族等民族的典籍作品。云南共有25个少数民族，其中11个少数民族的典籍作品都覆盖到了，不少作品还是首次译成英文。这将彻底改变云南少数民族典籍由于对外译介数量较少，不为世界了解的尴尬局面。

对于云南师范大学外国语学院而言，把少数民族典籍英译作为翻译专业的优势特色进行建设，这将对该院的学科建设起到助推作用。"云南少数民族经典作品英译文库"所产生的翻译成果和研究成果将培养出一批优秀的典籍翻译和研究团队，凸显该院在全国的学术特色和学术影响，同时还能将翻译能力和研究能力转化为教学能力，提高云南师范大学外国语学院翻译专业研究生的培养质量，为社会输送高水平的翻译人才，有力地支撑学院翻译专业学科的建设和发展。我对云南师范大学外国语学院的翻译师资队伍较为熟悉。作为云南省唯一获得省级高校优势特色学科建设项目的外国语学院，该院具有雄厚的翻译师资力量，在云南省各高校中当属第一。多年来，该院翻译与跨文化研究团队一直承担着对外交流与合作的各种口笔译项目及任务。由外国语学院精心挑选和确定的"云南少数民族经典作品英译文库"翻译人员绝大多数都是云南省翻译领域里的知名教授或专家，有国外留学经历，且具有扎实的英汉双语语言功底，曾翻译出版多部译著和翻译作品，并且主持和参与过多项翻译项目的研究。我阅读李昌银教授发来的文库翻译人员名单，发现多名我所熟悉的知名教授、博士也在其中，感到格外放心。

"云南少数民族经典作品英译文库"的出版发行是云南省翻译界的一件大事，也是我国少数民族典籍翻译传来的又一佳音。想当年，我和《大中华文库》总协调人李林老师曾在参加全国典籍英译学术研讨会之余一起找到李昌银教授，敦促李教授向学校和同事呼吁，少数民族典籍翻译及研究是富矿，值得快挖、深挖，能早出成果，出大成果。今天，我们当年的心愿变成了美好的现实，心里感到特别高兴。再次热烈祝贺"云南少数民族经典作品英译文库"的顺利出版！

（王宏，中国典籍翻译研究会副会长、苏州大学博士生导师）

Foreword by Wang Hong

My friend Professor Li Changyin of Yunnan Normal University asked me to write a few words for the publication of *Classics of Yunnan Ethnic Groups in English Translation*. I am more than delighted to do it. As I have been doing research in the English translation of Chinese classics, I know how important his work is. In recent years, substantial progress has been made in translating Chinese ethnic classics into English and other foreign languages. Books published in this respect include *The Liao Songs of the Zhuang Nationality* (Nanning: Guangxi Normal University Press, 2008, English Edition), *Mongolian Series: Jianggeer* (Changchun: Jilin University Press, 2012, Bilingual Edition), *Tibetan Gnomic Verses Translated into English* (Changchun: Changchun Press, 2013), and *Geser Khan: a Hero* (Changchun: Jilin University Press, 2014). Several projects in the English translation of ethnic classics have received funding from the National Planning Office of Philosophy and Social Science and, as a result, a number of monographs and PhD dissertations have been published.

Meanwhile, it is encouraging to see that the first conferences on English translation of ethnic classics in China have been held in Guangxi Nationalities University and

Dalian Nationalities Institute respectively. Participants were both many and enthusiastic. Many papers were presented and a lot of topics discussed. The third conference will be hosted by South Central Nationalities University in 2016.

Why, then, has this field attracted so much attention from translators and scholars alike and accomplished so much in just a few years? The answer, I believe, lies in a rethinking of what constitutes Chinese classics as an indispensable part of human heritage. We used to see Chinese classics as more or less equal to the classics of the Han people, excluding works by other ethnic groups. Moreover, when we talk about Chinese classics, we focus too much on the literary works of ancient times. Yet Chinese classics actually refer to "important works and books before 1911, the year when the Qing dynasty fell, bringing an end to imperial rule." This definition requires us to pay attention not just to literary works, but also writings in other subjects, such as philosophy, science, law, medicine, economics, military affairs, astronomy, and geography, not only Han works, but writings by other ethnic groups as well.

The classical works of a nation are its archetypal symbols, the major carriers of its cultural genes. Chinese classics make up the core of Chinese tradition. The Chinese nation consists of 56 ethnic groups. Ethnic classics are an important part of not only Chinese traditional culture, but also of world civilization. The translation of these works into other languages is important in that it helps to promote cross-cultural communications between China and other countries and to protect and preserve the uniqueness and diversity of ethnic cultures by making them accessible to foreign readers.

Chinese ethnic classics cover a variety of areas, such as religion, literature, history, language, medicine, astrology, and calendar, with numerous editions, special media and unique ways of transmission from generation to generation. Take, for example, *An Anthology of Chinese Ethnic Classics*, a colossal project that includes 110 volumes, 20 of which, from 23 ethnic groups, have been published. The anthology reflects the variety and quantity of China's ethnic classics and provides valuable material and resources for studying, understanding and developing Chinese culture and history in a more comprehensive and sustainable way.

The translation of Chinese ethnic classics into foreign languages is a very demanding job, involving rendering from ethnic languages to Chinese, between ethnic languages, and from ethnic languages (often via Chinese) to foreign languages. The first two types of translation can be traced back to the Spring and Autumn Period, when *The Song of the Yue People* was translated from their mother tongue into Chinese. The earliest translation of ethnic classics into a foreign language is *Wisdom of Royal Glory*, a long poem of the Uygurs, which was rendered from the source language into Arabic and is now in the Oriental Institute of Uzbekistan at Namangan. But it was not until modern times that the translation of ethnic classics into foreign languages accelerated. Noticeably, ethnic epics, such as *The Story of Prince Geser* of the Tibetans, *The Story of Jianggeer* of the Mongolians, *Manas* of the Kyrgyz, and narrative poems such as *Ashima* of the Yi people, *Alip and Salam* of the Uygurs, etc., have been published. These translations have contributed to acquainting the world with Chinese ethnic classics, but many remain to be translated.

Yunnan is rich in ethnic classics, boasting more than 100 thousand volumes of written classics and over 40 thousand pieces of oral literature. Relying on such bountiful resources, as a collective endeavor of the translation team of the School of Foreign Languages and Literature, Yunnan Normal University and with the help of Yunnan People's Publishing House, *Classics of Yunnan Ethnic Groups in English Translation* is the first project to translate Yunnan ethnic classics into English on a large scale. The School adheres to a professional spirit and academic standard in carrying out the project by selecting the most authoritative texts in the source language (Chinese) and recruiting the best translators from its huge faculty. The selection of the works, covering eleven of the twenty-five ethnic groups of the province, indicates expertise and insight. The implementation of the project will change the embarrassing obscurity of Yunnan ethnic classics by making them known to the world, many of them for the first time.

In light of disciplinary development, the project is of

great importance, too. Participating in the translation will strengthen the academic foundation of the teachers, enrich their experience and enhance their translation skills and research ability. This in turn will help them become better teachers and thus able to educate students with higher quality. The publication of the books will add greatly to the faculty accomplishments of the School and raise the academic standing of Yunnan Normal University by taking the first step in this direction among the universities of Yunnan province.

This publication project is a great event not only for Yunnan itself, but also for China. Looking back, I remember that Professor Li Changyin, our friend Li Lin, editor of the *Library of Chinese Classics*, and I talked enthusiastically about initiating something like this in Yunnan when we attended a conference on the translation of ethnic classics in Soochow. Lin and I strongly suggested that Professor Li do it as soon as possible. Now I am very pleased to see our talk becoming reality. Again, my congratulations on the publication of *Classics of Yunnan Ethnic Groups in English Translation*!

(Wang Hong, PhD supervisor at Soochow University, Vice Chairman of Classics Translation Committee of CACSEC)

General Introduction

This publication project, Classics of *Yunnan Ethnic Groups in English Translation*, aims at introducing Yunnan ethnic classical works to the world by making them available to native speakers of English who might be interested in them. With the publication of the *Library of Chinese Classics*, which consists only of books written by Han authors in classical Chinese, attention now is being turned to the English translation and publication of ethnic classics, books produced by ethnic writers about their history and culture. Universities in provinces such as Guangxi, Guizhou, Liaoning, Xinjiang, and Xizang, have taken the initiative. We in Yunnan must do something, because Yunnan has the largest number of ethnic groups in China. 15 of the 25 ethnic groups in the province, the Bai, the Dai, the Hani, the Lisu, the Wa, the Lahu, the Naxi, the Jingpo, the Bulang, the Pumi, the Achang, the Jinuo, the Nu, the De'ang, and the Dulong, live in no other place but Yunnan. The classics of these people, either in their own languages or in Chinese translations, are a great treasure house, which should be accessible to English readers and scholars. But what works should be translated first?

All the 25 ethnic groups in Yunnan have their classics, epics, mythology, creation stories, folksongs, folk drama, mountain songs, and funeral lament lyrics, most of which exist in different versions in different places. According to one estimation, there are more than 100 thousand volumes of them, excluding those in oral form. After a thorough survey and extensive consultations with experts of ethnic studies, we concluded that priority must be given to epics and mythologies, as they reflect an ethnic people's philosophy, history and culture more than anything else by narrating the stories of where and how they think they came from. From many epics and mythologies, we selected 17 of the most authoritative and popular classics representing 11 Yunnan ethnic groups, the Yi, the Bai, the Miao, the Hani, the Lahu, the Naxi, the Jingpo, the Pumi, the Achang, the Dai, and the De'ang. These works are all in Chinese, translated from the original by bilingual scholars whose mother tongue is their own ethnic language and who are fluent and proficient in Chinese. Some were recorded from their oral form at rituals and performances. We did not choose texts written in the ethnic language, not least because it is very hard to find a translator who is skilled in both the ethnic language and English. Moreover, some of the classics in the ethnic language were circulated in various oral forms and fragments. The published Chinese versions have been carefully edited and translated, hence they are more reliable. The next question is: how to translate them?

It happens that all of the 17 works except one are in

verse form, with lines more or less the same length and loose rhymes, but no regular meter. A poem must be rendered into a poem; anything less is unacceptable. So here are the general rules we follow when doing the translation.

One. If the original is verse, the translated text must be verse, too.

Two. Reproduce the ideas and the images of the original as completely as possible.

Three. Reproduce the figures of speech of the original as much as possible.

Four. Do not change the number of lines in a stanza unless absolutely necessary.

Five. Do not use standard meters in English, because the Chinese original does not follow any regular meter. Use the natural rhythm of English instead, but most of the lines should look more or less the same length.

Six. Do not use rhyme unless it comes naturally and is faithful to the content of the original.

What we try to do is, to use Susan Bassnett's words, "transplant the seed", not the tree itself. As for the various aspects of form, particularly meter and end rhyme, we reproduce them when it is possible and abandon them when it is necessary.

Who will do the translations? As this is a collective project of the School of Foreign Languages and Literature of Yunnan Normal University, our team consists of a dozen faculty members and two students from our MA translation program who are already teachers in other universities. All the translators have been teaching translation and doing translation research for a long time. They have published not just academic articles on translation, but also translated books from English to Chinese or vice versa.

Traditionally, people translate into their mother tongue, not into a foreign language. But the situation is changing. Many translators today are translating from their mother tongue into a foreign language. The quality can be good, as Nike K. Pokorn and Stuart Campbell prove in *Challenging the Traditional Axioms: Translation into a non-mother tongue* (Amsterdam: John Benjamins Publishing Company, 2005) and *Translation into the Second Language* (New York: Routledge, 2013) respectively. The case of China provides further evidence for their argument. The translation of Chinese classics into English was initiated by James Legge and Herbert Allen Giles in the 19th century and carried on in the 20th century by Arthur Waley, David Hawkes, Burton Watson, John Minford, Stephen Owen and others. It is noticeable that these English and American sinologists were soon joined by Chinese scholars residing in the West, such as Hongming (Tomson) Gu and Lin Yutang, among others. They took up the job because they thought it was their obligation to give English readers more faithful translations than Western sinologists could, who, as their target language is their mother tongue, often misinterpret the original text and misrepresent Chinese culture. Since the 1950s, there has been an increasingly powerful trend for Mainland Chinese translators to render or re-render Chinese classics into foreign languages, English in particular. In our time, this work is gathering momentum, enthusiastically advocated and actively practiced by such well-known translation experts as Yang Xianyi of Beijing Foreign Language Press, Xu Yuanchong of Beijing University, Wang Rongpei of Dalian Foreign Language Institute, Wang Hongyin of Nankai University, Wang Hong of Soochow University, Li Zhengshuan of Hebei Normal University, and many more. These professors are not just translators, but also scholars in translation studies. More importantly, some of them, Xu Yuanchong, Wang Hong and Li Zhengshuan, for example, have had their translations published by Western publishers, which suggests that their English meets the international standard.

In the case of our project, we request that the translators do their best to produce good translations. When they submit them to us, they should represent the highest level that they can attain. Then the general editors appointed by the School read the translated texts and remove inaccurate renderings and grammar mistakes if there are any. On top of that, we've taken an indispensable measure to ensure that our English is readable. We asked Ms. Joan Cecile Boulerice, an American teacher who has been teaching English in our school since

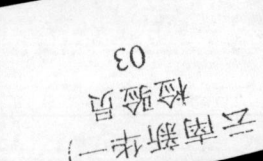

2009, to read every text that we've translated and improve the English by making it more natural and idiomatic. This is the best we can do. Of course any problems that still remain in the translations are ours. They have nothing to do with our American teacher.

As the project is well under way, we would like to thank all those who have helped to make it possible. Ms Guo Muyu, director of the South and Southeast Asia Editorial Department, Yunnan People's Publishing House, has been most helpful in our cooperation. In addition, she has added importance to the project by turning it into a national publication project. Yunnan Normal University has supported us by paying the publication fees so that the translators won't have to be burdened with the financial responsibilities for this project. Professor Li Zhengshuan and Professor Wang Hong not only have always encouraged us to go on but have also written the forewords for the project, putting it in a global perspective. Ms Joan Boulerice's revision has ensured the fluency of the translated texts. Finally, special thanks must be given to Professor Wang Hong, again, and Mr Li Lin of Hunan People's Press for their suggestion that has helped us conceive the project from the very beginning.

(The General Editors, School of Foreign Languages & Literature, Yunnan Normal University, Kunming)

A Brief Introduction to *Pamichali*

Pamichali is an important mythical genesis epic of the Pumi people and it is widely sung in Pumi communities. With the development of modernization and the gradual death of elderly singers, there are very few that can sing the entire epic now. Therefore, the content of the epic is widely spread among the Pumi people as stories.

The epic is divided into nine parts. The first part is called "Collecting Golden Light". It says that in the dark ages long long ago, a girl and her fourth brother became the sun and the moon because they wanted to collect golden light to illuminate the world. The second part is "Great Flood", which tells how the three brothers at home got to know that a great flood was coming and how the third brother survived the flood. The third part, "Uncle Frog", describes how the third brother survived the mouth of devils with the help of Uncle Frog. The fourth part, "Finding Fairies", describes how the third brother asked immortal Abodu to create human beings. Due to the third brother's anxiousness, Abodu's efforts were not successful. However, with the immortal Adodu's direction, the third brother managed to find the three Fairies. The fifth part is "Killing the Demon Bravely" which describes how the third brother helped the three fairies kill the demon. The sixth part is "The Hero Choosing His Bride", which tells the readers how the third brother chose the third immortal girl to be his bride. The seventh part, "God's Tests", describes how the third brother passed God Muduodingba's test with the help of the third immortal girl. Therefore, God allowed his third daughter to go to the mortal world with the third brother. The eighth part, "The Origin of Seeds" is about the origin of seeds and the multiplication of human beings.

This epic contains many common elements of creation narratives, such as the pursuit of light, a great flood, immortals, demons, multiplication of human beings, and the origins of many customs of the Pumi people. Therefore, the creation epic is an indispensable resource for studies in the history and culture of the Pumi people.

The Translator

目 录

采金光 // 1

洪水朝天 // 19

青蛙舅舅 // 43

寻找仙女 // 65

勇杀魔王 // 81

英雄选亲 // 95

天神的考验 // 111

种子的由来 // 123

Contents

Collecting Golden Light // 1

Great Flood // 19

Uncle Frog // 43

Finding Fairies // 65

Killing the Demon Bravely // 81

The Hero Choosing His Bride // 95

God's Tests // 111

The Origin of Seeds // 123

采金光

Collecting Golden Light

那是遥远的古代，
天上没有太阳，
也没有星星和月亮，
天空一片漆黑茫茫。

那是遥远的古代，
地上没有鸟语花香，
也没有五谷食粮，
大地一片漆黑茫茫。

不知过了多少年月，
突然有一道金光，
在天地间一划就熄灭，
它给世界带来了希望。

那是什么东西在发亮？
那闪耀金光来自何方？
那是海螺树在开花，
那金光来自遥远的东方。

在那遥远的东方，
有一片大海汪洋。
海边有棵海螺树，

In ancient time long, long ago,

There was no sun,

No star and no moon in the sky.

There was only complete darkness in the sky.

In ancient time long, long ago,

There was no birds' singing, no flowers' fragrance,

No grain and no food on the earth.

There was only complete darkness on the earth.

Nobody knows how many ages passed;

Suddenly a golden light

Flashed across the sky before it went out.

It brought hope to the world.

What gave off the light?

Where did the flashing golden light come from?

The golden light came from a conch tree blooming;

The golden light came from the faraway east.

In the faraway east,

There existed a big sea.

There was a conch tree beside the sea,

神奇的海螺花在开放。

那神奇的海螺花，
一万年才开一次，
花开时金光照亮天地，
转瞬就花谢光灭。

不知过了多少万年，
海螺花又复盛开，
一闪一闪的金光，
在东方的海边闪亮。

在离海边很远的地方，
居住着一户人家，
四个哥哥和一个妹妹，
在黑暗中裸体度着时光。

那海螺花开的金光，
一下子照亮了天地，
五个兄妹睁开了眼睛，
五个兄妹异常喜欢。

聪明的妹妹开口说：
"那金光来自东方，

And magic conch flowers were blooming.

The magic conch flowers
Only bloomed once in ten thousand years.
When they bloomed, golden light lit up the world.
But in a flash the flowers withered and the light went out.

Nobody knows how many ages passed
Before the conch flowers bloomed again.
Twinkling, twinkling golden light
Flashed in the eastern sky.

In a place faraway from the sea,
There lived a family.
Four brothers and one sister,
Lived in darkness and nakedness.

The golden light from the blooming conch flowers,
Illuminated the sky and the earth suddenly.
The five siblings opened their eyes;
All were extremely happy.

The clever sister said:
"The golden light comes from the east,

我要去把它采来，
把天和地永远照亮。"

四哥接着妹妹话：
"妹妹一人太孤单，
我和妹妹一起去，
采来金光照四方。"

大哥口气冷冰冰：
"你俩真是痴心妄想，
那金光原是神光，
谁也走不到它身旁。"

二哥说得更可怕：
"那金光原是阴光，
那阴光照阴不照阳，
哪个采了就活不长。"

只有三哥不一样：
"寻找光明要勇敢，
你俩采到了金光，
大地和天空都会被照亮。"

得到了三哥的鼓励，

And I will go to collect it
To illuminate the sky and the earth forever."

Then the fourth brother said:
"Our sister alone will be too lonely.
So I will go with her
To collect golden light to illuminate the world."

The eldest brother said coldly:
"You two are really daydreaming.
The golden light is a former divine light,
And nobody can go close to the light."

What the second brother said was even more frightening:
"The golden light is a former ghost light.
It is only illuminated for the dead rather than the living;
The people who collect it will die."

Only what the third brother said was different:
"People must be brave to seek for light.
If you two can bring back golden light,
The earth and the sky will be bright."

Encouraged by the third brother,

四哥和小妹信心更强。
告别了三位哥哥，
兄妹俩一起走向东方。

天上一片黑茫茫，
地上一片黑茫茫。
兄妹俩在黑暗中爬行，
艰难地一直爬向东方。

不知爬了多少年，
兄妹俩爬上了一座山尖。
到处是悬崖绝壁，
兄妹俩无法继续向前。

突然一个白发老奶奶，
出现在兄妹俩面前：
"你们兄妹俩要去哪里？
为何爬上这无路的山尖？"

妹妹礼貌地回答说：
"我们要去采金光，
采来金光照天地，
请求奶奶多指点。"

The fourth brother and the sister became more confident.

After saying goodbye to their brothers,

The brother and the sister set off toward the east.

The sky was completely dark;

The earth was equally dark.

The brother and the sister crawled in darkness,

Toward the east arduously.

No one knows how many years they crawled.

They finally climbed onto a peak,

And found they were surrounded by cliffs,

Unable to go forward any longer.

Suddenly a white-haired granny appeared,

In front of the brother and the sister.

"Where are you going young men?

Why do you come to this pathless peak?"

The sister replied politely:

"We want to collect the golden light,

To illuminate the sky and make the earth bright.

Dear granny, could you please give us some tips? "

白发奶奶笑着说：
"要采金光照天地，
永生永世不歇息，
这苦你们可吃得起？"

妹妹连忙回答说：
"要是怕吃苦受难，
我们就不会来到这里，
我们一定要采到金光！"

勇敢的哥哥接着说：
"只要能采到金光，
把黑暗的天地照亮，
就是死我们也甘愿！"

听了兄妹俩的话，
白发奶奶满心欢喜：
"如今天地一片漆黑，
我正在寻找照明的人。

"你们为了光明吃苦，
万物都要感谢你们。
哥哥白天出去照亮，
妹妹夜晚出去照明。"

The white-haired granny smiled,

"To collect the golden light to illuminate the world,

You can never have a rest.

Can you endure such hardship?"

The sister answered quickly:

"If we were afraid of hardship,

We would not have come here.

We must do our best to collect the golden light!"

The brave brother went on to say:

"As long as we can collect the golden light

To make the world bright,

We are willing to sacrifice our lives!"

Hearing the siblings' words,

The white-haired granny was very happy:

"Now the world is completely in darkness.

I am looking for people to illuminate it."

"If you can endure hardship to seek the light;

All the beings in the world will be grateful to you.

The brother will go to illuminate the world in the daytime;

And the sister will go at night."

白发奶奶吩咐完,
妹妹开口忙求情:
"我夜晚出去害怕,
让哥哥和我同行。"

白发奶奶摇头说:
"你和哥不能同行,
如果夜晚出去害怕,
你就白天出去照明。"

妹妹还是不答应:
"我没有穿着衣服,
白天光着身子出去,
怕人见了我害羞!"

白发奶奶拍拍妹妹:
"我给你一包绣花针,
哪个要是敢看你,
就用针刺他的眼睛。"

老奶奶给妹妹一把火,
妹妹当了金色的太阳。
她专门白天出来照亮,

After hearing what the white-haired granny said,

The sister immediately asked for a favor:

"I am afraid of going out at night.

Please allow my brother to go with me."

The white-haired granny shook her head and said:

"You and your brother can not go together.

If you are afraid of going out at night,

You can go out in the daytime instead."

The sister did not agree.

"Because I'm not dressed,

If I go out in the daytime naked,

I'll be ashamed of being seen by others!"

The white-haired granny patted on her shoulder,

"I will give you a packet of needles.

If anyone dares to look at you,

You can use the needles to dazzle his eyes. "

The granny gave the sister a torch,

And she became the golden sun.

She comes out to illuminate the world in the daytime,

从东方一直走到西方。

一直到了现在，
地上的人抬头看她，
她就撒出绣花针，
刺痛人家的眼睛。

老奶奶给哥哥一朵白花，
哥哥当了银色的月亮。
等妹妹走完了白天，
他夜晚才出来照亮。

天上有了太阳和月亮，
地上有了白天和夜晚。
树木和花草越长越多，
树林中有了各种动物。

地上的三位哥哥，
怕被天上的弟妹看见，
他们还赤身裸体，
就用兽皮穿在身上。

他们看见鸟儿搭窝，
就学着鸟儿的样，

And walks from the east to the west everyday.

Even up to now,

When people look at her,

She will use the needles,

To dazzle people's eyes.

The granny gave the brother a white flower,

And he became the silver moon.

After his sister works in the daytime,

He comes out to illuminate the world at night.

After the sun and the moon came into being,

People began to have daytime and nighttime.

More and more trees, flowers and grass began to grow,

And all kinds of animals appeared in the woods.

The three brothers on the earth

Were afraid that their brother and sister in the sky would see,

That they were still naked.

They began to dress themselves in fur.

They saw how birds built their nests,

And they learned from the birds,

用树枝搭起了住房，

生活在光明的大地上。

To build houses with branches.

They have lived on the bright land ever since.

洪水朝天
Great Flood

三个弟兄有了住房，
就开始砍林开荒。
他们要种好庄稼，
才对得起太阳和月亮。

砍倒茂密的丛林，
挖翻肥沃的黑土。
要撒播喷香的荞籽，
要撒播金色的麦种。

三弟兄都聪明勤劳，
三弟兄都身强力壮。
三弟兄一连开荒三天，
天天都有怪事出现。

头天砍倒的树木，
第二天去又站了起来；
头天翻挖过的荒地，
第二天去又全还了原。

这是魔鬼在施妖法，
成心不让人种好庄稼？
还是天神在作预兆，

Since the three brothers had houses to live in,

They began to cut bushes and reclaim wasteland.

They wanted to grow crops,

So as not to disappoint the sun and the moon.

They cut down dense bushes,

And cultivated fertile black soil.

They wanted to sow fragrant buckwheat seeds,

And golden wheat seeds with toil.

All three brothers were clever and diligent;

All three brothers were healthy and strong.

They reclaimed the land for three days on end,

But odd things happened everyday on their land.

The trees that had been cut down

Stood again the next day on the ground;

The wasteland that had been cultivated,

Recovered to its original state in the following day.

Was that caused by the magic of devils,

Who did not want people to grow crops?

Or was that a warning from God,

要有灾难降临人间？

弟兄们决心弄清原因，
免得成天心情惶惶。
他们又砍了一林树，
他们又开了一片荒。

到夜里三人全出动，
大哥拿着尖利的梭镖，
二哥拿着闪亮的大刀，
老三拿着一根木棒。

弟兄三人躲在老林里，
三个人守住四面八方。
竖着耳朵静静地听，
睁着眼睛细细地看。

二更过去没有动静，
三更过去没有异样。
三弟兄埋怨白守了一夜，
很快就要鸡叫天发亮。

莽莽老林里一片漆黑，
突然只听见一阵风响，

That disasters would befall the world?

The brothers decided to find the cause,

So as not to worry about it every day.

They cut some more trees,

And reclaimed one more piece of land.

At night all of them set out,

The eldest brother holding a sharp spear,

The second brother holding a sharp knife,

The third brother holding a wooden pole.

The three brothers hid in the forest,

Each at a different corner.

They listened attentively in silence,

And observed carefully and vigilantly.

Nothing happened in the second two-hour period;

Nothing unusual occurred in the third two-hour period.

The three brothers complained that they had waited in vain,

As the cocks would be crowing soon and daybreak was coming.

The dense forest looked totally dark.

Suddenly a wind blew past.

一只草墩大的青蛙，
驾着急风来到荒地上。

青蛙围着砍倒的树木，
左跳三下，右跳三下，
只听刷刷刷一片响，
砍倒的树木全站起来。

青蛙踩着深翻的荒地，
左抓三把，右抓三把，
只听呼呼呼山坡动，
深翻的荒地还了原。

虽是黑夜老林里，
三个弟兄看得清。
原是青蛙在作怪，
怪事原因已分明。

大哥挥着长梭镖，
怒气冲冲出老林：
"刺死这个老怪物，
原来是你在害人！"

二哥举起大砍刀，

A frog as big as a cushion,

Flew to the wasteland by a swift wind.

Around the cut-down trees,

The frog leaped leftward three times and rightward three times.

With a series of rustling sounds,

All the trees stood up.

The frog stood on the deeply-cultivated land,

Grasped three times leftward and three times rightward.

With a series of whirring sounds from the slope,

All the cultivated land recovered to its original state.

Though they were hiding in the dark forest,

The three brothers saw what happened.

The odd things were caused by the frog,

And the reasons were now clear.

Holding his long spear in the hand,

The eldest brother rushed out of the forest in a rage:

"I'll stab you to death, old monster,

Because it was you that made all the troubles."

Raising his big knife,

跳到面前更气愤：
　"把你砍成三半截，
看你还敢害我们？"

老三连忙跳过来，
举起木棒架大刀，
举起木棒架梭镖，
挡住哥哥忙求告：

　"先不忙杀不忙砍，
青蛙素来就聪明，
夜里来做这种事，
其中一定有原因。"

三个弟兄说话间，
青蛙蹲地变成了人：
一个白胡子老爷爷，
抹着胡子笑盈盈。

老三上前行过礼，
然后开口问底细：
　"我们从没得罪你，
老人家为何生大气？"

The second brother jumped to face the frog and shouted:
"After I cut you into three pieces,
Can you still harm us?"

The third brother rushed forward in a haste.
He raised his wooden pole to stop the knife
And the spear,
And spoke earnestly to save the frog's life:

"Do not cut and kill in haste.
Frogs are usually clever.
Since this frog is doing such things at night,
There must be some reasons."

While the three brothers were speaking,
The frog crouched down and changed into a person,
A white-bearded old man,
Holding his beard in his hand smiling.

The third brother bowed to him,
And then began to inquire:
"We never made trouble with you.
Why are you so angry elderly mister?"

青蛙变成的老爷爷，
摇着白胡子开了口：
"我看你是个善良人，
就把实话告诉你。

"三天后洪水要朝天，
你们不消再开荒地。
整个世界都要毁掉，
何消再开荒白费力！"

三天后世界要毁灭，
三弟兄一听着了急。
三人连忙跪下地，
齐向老爷爷讨生计。

"请问尊敬的老人家，
洪水朝天大灾来，
我们怎样能保命，
我们怎样来躲避？"

老人本来不泄密，
可看在老三的情分上，
白胡子老倌说秘密，
白胡子老倌道天机。

While holding his white beard in his hand,

The elderly man, the former frog, said :

"I think you are a kind person,

So I'll tell you the truth."

"Because the flood will rise sky-high in three days,

You don't need to reclaim the wasteland.

The whole world will be ruined,

And it's no use laboring on the land!"

Hearing that in three days the world would be destroyed,

The three brothers became worried.

They knelt on the ground,

To beg the old man for ideas to survive.

"Respected old mister,

When the disaster of the sky-high flood arrives,

How can we save our lives?

How can we find a place to hide?"

The old man did not intend to tell the secret.

But for the sake of the third brother's kindness,

The white-bearded old man began to tell secrets,

—The secrets of heaven.

"洪水朝天是劫难，
地上万物难逃避。
只有巴扎甲楚崩①，
这棵神树能化吉。

"老大拴在树底下，
老二拴在树半腰，
老三拴在树尖尖，
各人的位置要记好。

"老三再缝个牛皮袋，
装进猫狗和公鸡，
再装黑黄白石共三块，
大粑粑装上二十七个。"

"神雕的大窝在树梢，
你就躲在它窝里……"
老人将秘密传老三，
授完天机便无踪迹。

再过三天洪水就朝天，
再过三天世界就毁灭。
三弟兄按青蛙的吩咐，

_____
① 巴扎甲楚崩：即高大无比的神树，与天地同生。

"The sky-high flood is a catastrophe;

It's difficult for all living things on the land to survive.

Only Ba-zha-jia-chu-beng, the holy tree,

Can save your lives."

"The eldest brother is to be attached to the trunk of the tree,

The second brother to the central part of the trunk,

And the third brother at the top of the tree.

You must remember your positions clearly."

"The third brother should sew a cowhide bag,

Put in a cat, a dog and a cock,

And three black, three yellow, and three white stones,

And put in twenty-seven big griddle cakes."

"The nest of the holy eagles is at the top of the tree,

And you can hide in it... "

The old man told the third brother the secret,

And then disappeared.

Three days later the flood would rise sky-high;

Three days later the world would be destroyed.

Following the instructions of the frog,

急忙把一切准备就绪。

那注定的时刻来到了，
凶猛的洪水朝天涌起。
轰隆轰隆像天崩地裂，
轰隆轰隆一片昏天黑地。

世界成了一片汪洋，
大地成了深深的海底。
洪水还在不断地涨高，
像要把天地连成一体。

老三爬到神树尖上，
躲在神雕的大窝里。
他什么也看不清楚，
便心急火燎地问消息：

"大哥我害怕得很，
洪水涨到了哪里？"
"洪水已淹了我的脚跟。"
许久才传来微弱的回声。

过了一会老三又问：
"大哥洪水涨到了哪里？"

The three brothers prepared everything in order.

The destined moment finally arrived,

And the vicious flood began to rise.

It sounded like the crack of the earth and the collapse of the world;

With a loud noise there was no more light.

The world became a sea;

The land was flooded and became the bottom of the sea.

The flood was still rising,

As if to merge the sky with the earth into one body.

The third brother climbed to the top of the holy tree,

And hid in the nest of the holy eagles.

Unable to see anything,

He anxiously asked for information:

"My eldest brother, I am very scared.

Where is the flood now?"

"The flood has covered my heels."

A weak reply was heard after a long time.

Moments later the third brother asked again:

"My eldest brother, where is the water now?"

"洪水已淹了我的脖颈。"
大哥的回声惊魂不定。

老三第三次再问，
大哥早已没了回声。
大哥送命在洪水中，
老三更加胆战心惊。

他又焦急地问二哥：
"二哥洪水涨到了哪里？"
半天才传来恐怖的回声：
"洪水已淹了我的脖颈！"

一排巨浪轰响而来，
洪水又吞了二哥的命。
很快洪水猛涨上来，
淹没了老三的腰身。

老三想起了青蛙的话，
忙将黑石头朝水中抛。
黑石头落水叮咚响，
洪水马上退落到树腰。

老三见水退得快，

"The flood has risen to my neck."
The eldest brother replied in panic.

When the third brother asked for the third time,
The eldest brother had no response.
Knowing the eldest brother had lost his life in the flood,
The third brother became more scared.

He anxiously asked the second brother:
"My second brother, where is the water now?"
A long time later a horrified response came :
"The water has risen to my neck!"

A huge wave came roaring,
And it swallowed the second brother and took his life.
The flood rose violently,
And came up to the third brother's waist.

The third brother remembered the frog's words,
And threw a black stone into the water,
Which produced a "Ding-Dong" sound,
And the water immediately retreated to middle of the trunk.

The third brother saw the water retreating quickly,

连忙又丢那黄石头。
黄石头落水叮咚响，
洪水接着退落到树蔸。

老三再丢下白石头，
这回不听水声响。
只听见石头碰石头，
眼看洪水全退完。

老三丢下大公鸡，
公鸡落地喔喔啼。
洪水后一片大地茫茫，
地面上全是烂稀泥。

老三丢下小黄狗，
黄狗落地汪汪叫。
大山从地面升起来，
峡谷从地面落下去。

老三丢下小灰猫，
猫儿落地喵喵叫。
高山峡谷变完后，
又有了一块块平坝地。

And he quickly dropped a yellow stone.

When the sound of "Ding-Dong" came back,

The flood retreated to the root of the tree.

The third brother then threw a white stone.

This time he did not hear the sound of water;

He only heard the sound of stones colliding.

It seemed that the flood had retreated completely.

The third brother dropped the cock,

Which began to crow when it landed on the ground.

After the flood a vast land was left,

And everything was covered with mud.

The third brother dropped the little yellow dog,

Which began to bark when it landed on the ground.

The sun rose from the horizon,

And valleys appeared when the mud retreated.

The third brother dropped the little gray cat,

Which began to mew when landing on the ground.

After mountains and valleys appeared,

Then many many pieces of flatland began to appear.

朝天的洪水已过去，
鸡狗和猫全下了地，
皮袋里的粑粑也吃完，
老三心里却更着急。

这神树高得连着天，
在树尖上看不着地。
老三虽然保了命，
却无法下到地上去。

这天早上出了太阳，
神雕窝里一片光亮。
老雕叼回一只马鹿，
慈爱地放在小雕身旁。

饥饿无比的老三，
和小雕把鹿肉争抢。
待老雕又欲飞去，
吃饱的老三已有主张。

他抓住两根马鹿骨头，
飞快地骑到了神雕背上。
他要让翅膀三丈的神雕，
带他下树回到地上。

The sky-high flood had gone;

The chicken, dog and cat had landed on the ground.

When all the griddle cakes in the bag had run out,

The third brother became even more panicked.

The holy tree was as high as the sky;

From the canopy he could not see the ground.

Though he had survived the flood,

He could not get to the ground.

When the sun rose in the morning,

The nest of the holy eagles was full of sunlight.

A big eagle brought back a dead red deer,

And put it lovingly beside the chicks.

The third brother was very hungry;

He competed with the chicks for the venison.

When the holy eagle was going to fly away,

The satiated third brother already had an idea.

Holding two red deer bones,

He jumped onto the back of the holy eagle.

He would make the eagle with ten-meter-wide wings,

Bring him back to the ground.

神雕一飞几万里，
背上的老三又怕又急。
他不停地用马鹿骨头，
使劲敲打神雕的背脊。

巨大的神雕被打痛了，
开始渐渐地飞慢飞低。
最后落到山顶上歇气，
老三就这样回到了大地。

The holy eagle could fly tens of thousands of kilos without stop;

On its back the third brother was scared and worried.

He used the bones of the red deer,

To strike the back of the eagle.

His strike made the huge eagle hurt;

It gradually flew slowly and closer to the ground.

Finally it landed on a summit to have a rest;

The third brother thus came back to the ground.

青蛙舅舅

Uncle Frog

老三骑雕回到了大地，
他从山顶上走下山梁。
洪水之后的大地，
四面八方一片荒凉。

老三从东走到西，
茫茫大地寻不见个伙伴，
只有自己的影子跟着他，
一个人格外地凄凉孤单。

老三从南走到北，
眼睛睁得又痛又酸。
找不到一丁点食物，
肚子饿得腿软心慌。

老三饿得爬不动坡，
就专门朝着坡下走。
他走进一条阴森的峡谷，
来到一个很大的岩洞口。

看见两个妖怪在吃东西，
他俩面对面坐着，
你吃一口递给我，

The third brother came back to the ground by riding the eagle;

He then came down the ridge from the summit.

On the land after the flood,

Every corner was desolate.

The third brother walked from east to west,

But nobody could be found on the vast land.

Only his shadow was with him;

Being the only person, he felt especially lonely.

The third brother walked from south to north,

His eyes wide open and painful.

Unable to find anything to eat,

He became hungry, weak and panicked.

The third brother was too hungry to climb slopes;

He chose to walk down slopes.

He walked into a gloomy valley,

And came to the entrance of a big cave.

He saw two devils eating,

Sitting face to face.

One had a bite and passed the food to the other;

我吃一口又递给你。

两个妖怪长得丑陋骇人，
身上只有一只独脚，
那上眼皮却长得出奇，
从眼睛上一直拖盖到地上。

老三肚子太饿了，
顾不得怕那妖怪的丑脸。
他大着胆子摸过去，
悄悄站到两个妖怪中间。

左边的男妖把东西递过来，
老三接着吃掉了；
右边的女妖把东西递过来，
老三也接着吃掉了。

不见对方把东西递来，
两个妖怪都觉得奇怪。
妖怪同时问对方：
　"怎么不把东西递来？"

两个妖怪一起问完，
两个妖怪一起回答：

The other one had a bite and passed it back.

The two devils were terribly ugly,

Each having only one foot,

But extremely long upper eyelids,

which extended from their eyes to the ground.

The third brother was too hungry

To notice the devils' ugly faces.

He crept toward them boldly,

And stood between them silently.

When the left devil passed the food rightward,

The third brother accepted it and swallowed it;

When the right devil passed the food leftward,

The third brother accepted that and ate it too.

Without food being passed back,

Both devils felt strange.

They asked each other at the same time:

"Why don't you pass me the food?"

When the two monsters are finished,

Both answered at the same time:

"早都递过来了，
你全吃了还要问？"

男妖怪皱皱鼻子说：
"我怎么闻着生人味！
不信你也闻一闻，
莫非有人来捣鬼？"

女妖扭扭身子笑：
"洪水已经朝过天，
大地上哪里还有人？
不信我们来睁眼看。"

女妖边说边动手，
用木棍撑开了长眼皮，
看见老三在身边，
正狼吞虎咽地吃东西。

原来真有生人来，
女妖一见怒火起，
女妖连忙张血口，
一口将老三吞肚里。

女妖刚刚吞下人，

"I have passed it to you long ago.

Why do you ask me now that you have had it?"

The male devil sniffed and said:

"I can smell a stranger!

If you do not believe, you can sniff too.

Is it possible that someone has come here to make trouble?"

The female devil shook her body and laughed:

"The great flood rose sky-high.

It is impossible to have any humans on earth.

If you do not believe me, we can open our eyes to have a look."

While speaking the female devil started

To use a wooden pole to open her eyes.

She saw the third brother by her side

Eating like a wolf.

Seeing that there really was a stranger,

The female devil flew into a rage.

She opened her bloody mouth,

And swallowed the third brother into her stomach.

Just when the female devil had devoured the person,

洞里的石磨便停歇。
推磨的青蛙歇了手，
眼睛里不停滚泪滴。

妖怪觉得很奇怪：
青蛙推磨从不歇，
今天为何生了气？
连忙开口问仔细。

"青蛙有何伤心事
为何把磨来停歇？
不推粮食吃不成饭，
青蛙快把磨推起。"

男妖催了女妖催，
青蛙就是不动手。
青蛙走到女妖前，
流着眼泪开了口：

"刚才你吃的那人，
他是我的好外甥。
外甥老远来看我，
未见舅舅被你吞。

The stone mill in the cave stopped.

The frog stopped pushing the mill,

And burst into tears.

The devils felt strange,

As the frog had never stopped his work.

Why was he sad today?

They immediately asked the question.

"Frog, what are you sad for?

Why have you stopped pushing the mill?

If you don't push the mill we won't have food to eat.

Frog, be quick to continue to push the mill."

The male devil and the female devil urged him,

But the frog just refused to proceed.

The frog walked to face the female devil,

And with tears he opened his mouth:

"The person you swallowed just now,

Is my sister's son.

He came a long way to see me,

But he was swallowed by you before meeting me."

"你快把他吐出来，
让我们甥舅叙别情。
还我外甥我推磨，
不还外甥你请别人。"

青蛙说出情由来，
男妖听了不说话，
女妖听了跳独脚，
怒火冲冲吼青蛙：

"小小青蛙你好糊涂，
自从洪水朝天后，
好久未得吃人肉，
我连人骨都不吐。

"推磨的人到处有，
东有喜鹊三千五，
西有乌鸦五千六，
还有那多蟒蛇不算数。"

女妖说话口气硬，
坚决不吐肚里的人。
推磨的青蛙脾气怪，
掉头甩手出了门。

"You must get him out,

So that uncle and nephew can meet.

Return me my nephew and I'll push the mill.

Or you have to ask someone else. "

Hearing what the frog said,

The male devil kept silent.

The female devil jumped with her only foot,

And shouted at the frog in a rage:

"Little frog, how silly you are!

Since the sky-high flood,

I haven't had any human flesh and blood.

I do not even spit human bones this time.

I can find others to push the mill everywhere.

In the east there are three thousand and five hundred magpies;

In the west there are five thousand and six hundred crows,

And many serpents not included."

The female devil's mood was very harsh,

And she was determined not to spit out the person.

The mill-pushing frog had a bad temper.

He turned around and walked out of the cave.

妖怪请了喜鹊来，
喜鹊歇在磨盘上，
叽叽喳喳叫不停，
石磨丝毫无声响。

妖怪请了乌鸦来，
乌鸦歇在磨盘上，
啄住磨把拼老命，
石磨丝毫无声响。

妖怪请了蟒蛇来，
蟒蛇缠在磨盘上，
连着磨槽都堆满，
石磨仍然无声响。

男妖饿得眼发花，
淌着口水把妖婆骂：
"石磨不推要饿死，
还不快去请青蛙！"

女妖赶快出山洞，
跳着独脚上山尖。
青蛙算定她会来，

The devils invited magpies,

Which stood on the millstone,

And chirped, chirped without stop,

But the millstone did not move at all.

The devils then invited crows,

Which stopped on the millstone,

And pecked the handle of millstone and tried their best,

But the millstone stayed still and quiet.

The devils invited a serpent,

Which wrapped itself around the millstone,

And its body filled the groove of the mill.

But the millstone was still quiet.

The male devil was so hungry that he began to see stars,

And he cursed the female devil with saliva:

"If nobody pushes the millstone, we will die of hunger.

Why don't you go to invite the frog at once! "

The female devil quickly went out of the cave.

With her only foot she jumped step by step to the mountain top.

The frog was sure she would come,

青蛙本来就没走远。

青蛙看见女妖来，
站在路边不理她。
女妖见了青蛙面，
连忙笑口夸青蛙：

"还是青蛙会推磨，
还是青蛙力气大。
还是请你回洞去，
你要什么都好说话。"

青蛙还想着被吃的人，
青蛙还是很伤心。
听了女妖的奉承话，
青蛙口气更加硬：

"好话说尽都无用，
要我推磨快吐人。
还我外甥我推磨，
不还外甥你请别人。"

为求青蛙去推磨，
女妖答应吐外甥。

And he did not go far away.

Seeing the female devil coming,

The frog stood beside the road and ignored her.

When the female devil saw the frog,

She promptly smiled and praised the frog:

"You are the best to push the millstone;

You are still the strongest.

I'd like to ask you to come back to the cave,

And anything you want is negotiable."

The frog was concerned about the swallowed person;

The frog was still very sad.

Hearing the flattering remarks of the devil,

The frog's tone became even harder.

"It's useless to say anything flattering.

If you want me to push the millstone for you,

You have to spit out the person.

Return my nephew, or you have to ask others."

In order to persuade the frog to push the millstone,

The female devil agreed to spit out his nephew.

女妖实在无办法，
只好开口说真话：

"吃人我倒很容易，
吐人却要受苦罪。
你灌我九桶灶灰水，
再用石头砸我的背。"

九桶灶灰水灌下去，
一块石头砸上背。
女妖拼命呕吐开，
老三一下被吐出嘴。

只是还不见大耳朵，
又灌下三桶灶灰水，
青蛙又叫她继续吐，
石头又朝她背上捶。

女妖呕破黄苦胆，
吐出碎肉几点点，
女妖随便捏两下，
粘在人的头两边。

原来的人耳大又圆，

She had no other choice,

And told the truth:

"It's easy for me to swallow a person,

But it's suffering to throw a person up.

Use nine buckets of ash water as my gastric lavage water,

And strike my back with a stone."

Nine buckets of ash water were poured in,

And a stone was used to strike her back.

The female devil tried hard to vomit,

And the third brother was spit out of her mouth.

But his big ears were still missing,

So three more buckets of ash water were poured in.

The frog demanded her to continue to vomit,

And used a stone to strike her back again.

The female devil even spit out her bile,

But only some small pieces of meat were spit out.

The female devil casually sculpted the meat,

And attached it to both sides of the third brother's head.

Human beings' ears had formerly been big, round,

生在头上多好看。
那次妖怪重捏后，
才坑坑洼洼不美观。

原来的脚趾和手指，
个个长得一样长。
化在妖肚里的吐不出，
才长短不齐变了样。

丑恶的妖怪太凶残，
老三在她肚里受够了难。
好在老三还活着，
青蛙领他出了妖房。

青蛙为外甥指生路，
青蛙把办法教老三：
"你不要从峡谷头走，
那是妖怪住的地方。

"你要去找好心的神仙，
神仙住在冒烟的高山。
现在地上只有你一个人，
神仙会帮你把人类发展。"

And beautiful on human heads.

After the devil's remolding,

They become ugly and full of bumps and hollows.

Formerly human toes and fingers,

Had been equally long.

Because parts of them melted in the devil's stomach,

They have irregular length.

The ugly devil was too vicious;

The third brother suffered a lot in her stomach.

Fortunately he was still alive;

The frog led him out of the devils' cave.

In order to help his nephew to survive,

The frog taught the third brother a method:

"Do not go through the valley,

As it is the place where devils live."

"You should go to find the kindhearted immortals,

Who live on the foggy peaks.

You are the only person on the earth now;

The immortals may help you produce human beings."

老三跪在青蛙面前，
感谢舅舅的救命深恩：
    "世上最大的是舅舅，
我永远把舅舅尊敬！"

老三的后代也记住了恩情，
见了青蛙要让路叫舅舅。
普米人尊敬青蛙的规矩，
从那时一直流传至今。

The third brother knelt in front of the frog,

To show gratitude for saving his life:

"The most important one in the world is maternal uncle,

And I will always respect you, my maternal uncle!"

The third brother's descendants also remember his gratitude;

They give way to and greet uncles when they meet.

The Pumi tradition of respecting frogs,

Started from then.

寻找仙女
Finding Fairies

老三按青蛙舅舅的吩咐，
爬向青烟缭绕的高山。
到了青烟缭绕的山巅，
那是神仙阿波独的家园。

"尊敬的阿波独大神，
大地上遭了洪水的灾难，
人类只剩下了我一个，
请你帮助人类发展！"

阿波独听了老三的话，
看着他孤单单非常同情：
"你一个人太可怜了，
我尽力帮助你孤单的人！"

阿波独给他九根阳花木[①]，
阿波独给他九朵山茶花。
告诉他拿去插在地上，
告诉他九天以后去呼喊。

阳花木会变成九个男子，
山茶花变成九个女郎。
九男九女配成对，

① 阳花木：即杜鹃树。

Following the frog uncle's instructions,

The third brother climbed onto a foggy peak.

When he arrived at the fog-cloaked summit,

He came to the home of Abodu the immortal.

"Respected immortal Abodu,

The land suffered from a flood disaster,

And I am the only person alive.

Please help me to produce human beings!"

Hearing the third brother's words,

Abodu was sympathetic to the lonely person.

"You are pitiful to be the only person,

And I'll do my best to help you lonely person!"

Abodu gave him nine rhododendrons trees,

And nine camellia flowers.

He told him to plant them in the soil,

And to awaken them nine days later.

The rhododendrons trees would become nine men,

And the camellia flowers would become nine women.

When nine men match nine women,

人类就能重新发展。

老三记住神仙的话，
欢欢喜喜找个好地方，
插下了九根阳花木，
插下了九朵山茶花。

时间才过了三天，
老三觉得像过了三年。
他实在受不住孤寂了，
日夜守着看花木演变。

他忘记了神仙的嘱咐，
他忍不住发出了呼喊：
"醒来吧我的伙伴，
醒来吧美丽的姑娘！"

孤单的老三过分心急，
焦急的老三不该提前。
花木才插下地三天，
神仙的法术还不灵验。

九根阳花木伸了伸手，
九朵山茶花眨了眨眼。

Human beings would be produced again.

Keeping the immortal's words in mind,

The third brother happily found a good place.

He planted nine rhododendrons trees,

And nine camellia flowers.

Only three days passed,

But the third brother felt it was as long as three years.

He really could not stand the loneliness,

So he watched the changes of the flowers and the trees day and night.

He forgot the immortal's instructions;

He could not help calling:

"Wake up my peers;

Wake up beautiful girls!"

The lonely third brother was too anxious.

He should not awaken them ahead of time.

The trees and flowers had been planted for only three days,

And the immortal's magic was not yet effective.

The nine rhododendrons trees stretched their hands;

The nine camellia flowers only winked their eyes.

心急的老三坏了事，
变人的花木无法变全。

青翠的阳花木枯死，
鲜艳的山茶花蔫掉。
心急的老三懊悔不及，
只好又去把神仙求告。

阿波独骂他太心急，
阿波独又把新法教。
这回花木不能变人了，
只好另把路子寻找。

"你去找天神木多丁巴，
他有三个美丽的姑娘。
你娶个仙女回到人间，
人类就能重新得到发展。"

谢过了好心的神仙，
老三爬向了更远的高山。
去寻找遥远的天庭，
去求天神恩赐良缘。

他来到一座巍峨的高山，

The anxious third brother made serious mistakes;

The trees and flowers could not turn into human beings completely.

The green rhododendrons trees dried up and died;

The fresh camellia flowers withered.

The anxious third brother regretted this very much;

He was forced to beg to the immortal again.

Abodu criticized him for his anxiousness,

And gave him a new idea.

This time the trees and flowers could not become human beings;

He had to find other methods.

"You can go to see the God Muduodingba,

Who has three beautiful daughters.

If you can marry one of the girls,

Human beings can increase again.

After thanking the goodhearted immortal,

The third brother went toward the faraway mountains.

He went to seek for heaven,

To ask God for gifting a happy match.

He came to a towering mountain,

看见了一座堂皇的宫殿。
老三大胆地推门进去，
屋子里一个人影不见。

只见屋里一张桌子上，
摆着满满的清水三碗。
老三正走得腰酸腿痛，
老三正渴得嗓子冒烟。

老三将三碗清水，
一口气喝个碗底朝天。
喝饱清水好舒畅，
老三睡着在火铺下面。

人类在洪水中灭亡了，
灾难过后的大地上，
木多丁巴天天看见，
只有妖魔鬼怪在猖狂。

天神派他的三个女儿，
来到灾难过后的大地上，
要把妖怪全部杀尽，
要把魔鬼全部除光。

And saw a grand palace.

Boldly he pushed open the door and went in,

But there wasn't a single soul in the palace.

He saw a table in the room,

And three bowls of clear water were on the table.

The third brother was exhausted after a long journey;

He also had a sore throat due to thirst.

The third brother drank all the water in the bowls;

Not one drop of water was left.

He felt at ease and happy after drinking the water;

He fell asleep under the bed beside the fireplace.

Human beings became extinct in the flood.

On the land after the flood,

What God Muduodingba saw every day,

Were only devils and monsters roaming on the land.

God sent his three daughters,

To go to the disaster-stricken land,

To kill all devils,

And wipe out all monsters.

山上这座堂皇的宫殿，
就是三位仙女的住房。
她们和妖魔打仗去了，
凉了三碗神水放在桌上。

金色的太阳落下西山，
荒凉的山野暮色苍茫。
杀妖斗魔恶战了一天，
三位仙女一起回返。

姐妹三人进了屋，
来到桌前齐惊喊：
"难道是有妖怪来，
我的凉水被喝光！"

大姐说："有生人味，
不像妖怪像是人。"
二姐说："洪水灭了种，
大地上哪里还有人！"

三妹说："有个男人那倒好，
正好陪我们三姐妹。"
三妹说完姐姐笑，
姐妹三人笑成一团。

The grand palace on the mountain,

Was the place where the three fairies lived.

They had gone to fight against monsters,

And they left three bowls of magic water on the table.

The golden sun set behind western mountains,

Wild mountains full of twilight.

After fighting against devils the whole day,

The three fairies came back together.

The three sisters came into the room,

And shouted in surprise at the same time at the table:

"Have devils been here?

My water is gone!"

The eldest sister said, "There is the smell of a stranger.

It smells like a person rather than a devil."

The second sister said, "The flood has killed all human beings.

It's impossible to have a person here!"

The third sister said, "It'll be good if there is a man,

Because he can keep us company."

Hearing what she said, they all laughed,

And rolled on the floor.

欢声笑语满屋飞，

惊醒了床下睡觉的人。

老三听了三妹的话，

忍不住咕咕笑出声。

听见床下有笑声，

三位仙女齐喝问：

"谁在床下笑我们，

你快出来饶你的命！"

老三听了仙女的话，

连忙在床下说分明：

"好心的姑娘莫怪我，

我无衣遮羞怎见人！"

大姐听了老三的话，

挥手丢下一匹麻，

顺势吹一口仙气，

麻布变成了漂亮的衣裳。

二姐听了老三的话，

挥手丢下一匹麻，

顺势吹一口仙气，

Cheerful chatting and laughter filled the palace,

And woke up the person sleeping under the bed.

Hearing what the third sister said,

The third brother could not help chuckling.

Hearing laughter from under the bed,

The three fairies shouted in chorus:

"Who is under the bed and laughing at us?

Come out quickly and we can pardon your life."

The third brother heard the fairies' words,

And quickly answered from under the bed:

"Kindhearted girls, don't blame me.

I'm not dressed, how can I come out and meet you?"

The eldest sister heard what he said;

She threw out a bolt of linen,

And gave it a puff.

The linen became beautiful clothes.

The second sister heard what he said,

She drew out a bolt of linen,

And gave it a puff.

麻布变成了威风的头帕。

三妹听了老三的话，
挥手丢下一匹麻，
顺势吹一口仙气，
变成了鞋子和绑腿。

老三在床下穿好衣服，
神气活现地走出火铺。
一见这英俊的小伙子，
三姐妹高兴得欢跳起舞。

"我们以为人类灭绝了，
想不到还有一个活着。
你就不要再走了，
留下来和我们一起生活。"

The linen became a majestic head scarf.

The third sister heard what he said,

She drew out a bolt of linen,

And gave it a puff.

It became shoes and leg wrappings.

The third brother put on the clothes,

And came out from under the bed–very impressive.

Seeing the handsome young man,

The three sisters were excited.

"We thought human beings were extinct.

We never expected that you are still alive.

So don't leave here.

You can stay here and live with us."

勇杀魔王

Killing the Demon Bravely

妖魔鬼怪心肠黑，
妖魔鬼怪太凶险。
三位仙女为除魔，
天天忙着把箭练。

这天姐妹又练箭，
老三无事看一边。
三个仙女问老三：
"小伙是否会射箭？"

老三笑着把口开：
"以前打猎常射箭，
只怕好久不练习，
如今手脚不灵便。"

大姐递给他一张弓，
二姐递给他一壶箭。
三妹一旁笑着说：
"请你射了试试看。"

老三接过弓和箭，
正有只斑鸠飞蓝天。
只听一声急风响，

The Demon was too bad;

The Demon was too ferocious.

In order to wipe out the Demon,

The three sisters practiced archery every day.

One day when the sisters were practicing archery again,

The third brother watched them nearby.

The fairies asked him:

"Young man, can you shoot an arrow?"

The third brother said with a smile:

"I used to shoot arrows in hunting.

I haven't practiced archery for a long time.

I'm afraid I'm not very skillful now."

The eldest sister handed him a bow;

The second sister handed him a quiver of arrows;

The third sister said with a smile:

"Please have a try. "

When he accepted the bow and arrows,

One turtledove was flying in the blue sky.

With a whistle,

老三手中的箭离弦。

斑鸠应声落在地，
三个姐妹争着捡，
三妹一把抢在手，
两扇嘴壳一箭穿。

三个仙女齐喝彩，
从此一起把箭练。
老三眼亮心灵巧，
箭术越来越精练。

老三箭术进展快，
三个仙女大欢喜。
三人各拿一根针，
又叫老三来试箭。

三颗针儿插一排，
三个仙女站一边。
若是老三本事大，
三个针孔一箭穿。

老三不慌又不忙，
老三拉弓箭离弦。

The arrow in his hand left the bowstring.

The turtledove fell to the ground,

And the three sisters rushed to pick it up.

The third sister caught it first,

And found the arrow shot through its beak.

The three fairies cheered.

They began to practice archery with him.

The third brother had good eyesight and a smart mind,

So his archery became better and better with practice.

The third brother's archery improved fast,

And the three fairies were overjoyed.

They each held a needle in their hands,

And asked the young man to test his archery.

Three needles were arranged in a row,

Three fairies standing beside.

If the young man's archery was great,

His arrow would go through the eyes of the three needles.

The third brother did not hurry;

He pulled the bowstring and then shot the arrow.

不左不右正中间，
三个针孔一箭穿。

三个仙女心欢喜，
战胜魔王有希望。
老三箭术已高强，
可去出战杀魔王。

老三愿意去杀魔，
老三喜欢去出战。
可不知妖怪在哪里，
可不知魔王在哪方。

三个仙女讲战况，
姐妹三人说端详：
"小妖小怪已除尽，
只剩魔王在逞强。

"翻过这座高山去，
那边山下两个海；
一个海水像锅烟，
一个海水像牛奶。

"白海是吉祥的精灵，

Neither left nor right but in the center,

The arrow went through three eyes.

The three fairies were excited,

As it was hopeful they could defeat the Demon.

The third brother's archery was already excellent;

He could go to kill the Demon.

The third brother was willing to kill the Demon,

And he liked to fight against the Demon.

But he did not know where the Demon was,

And he did not know how to find it.

The three fairies told him the conditions;

The three sisters told him the details:

"All minor devils have been wiped out by us;

Only the Demon is still at large."

"After climbing this mountain,

You'll find two lakes at the other side of the mountain.

The water in one lake looks like soot;

The water in the other lake looks like milk.

"The white lake is the embodiment of the auspicious spirit,

黑海是邪恶的化身。
白海和黑海交战多时，
可至今还胜负难分。

"白海和黑海定好了，
明天还要进行较量。
明天你去参加交战，
你坐在两个大海的界边。

"白色海浪翻涌起，
你念颂如意吉祥。
黑色海浪翻涌时，
你赶快张弓搭箭。

"黑浪中会涌出匹黑马，
黑马驮着个黑色大汉。
那凶恶的大汉胸前，
旋转着一斑透亮的光点。

"当那大汉骑着黑马，
凶猛地扑向白色海浪，
你就射他胸前的光点，
射中光点魔魂就归天。"

While the black lake is the embodiment of evil.

The white lake and the black lake have been fighting for a long time,

But neither of them have won the battle."

"The white lake and the black lake have decided

To fight again tomorrow.

You can go to participate in the fight,

And you can wait between the lakes."

"When the white waves rise up,

You should recite the auspicious words.

When the black waves rise up,

You should pull your bowstring and aim your arrow."

"In the midst of the black waves there will be a black horse,

And a black man will be on the black horse.

On the chest of the vicious black man,

A bright light will be rotating. "

"When the black man riding the black horse,

Flies at the white waves,

You should shoot at the bright spot on his chest.

The Demon will die if you can shoot at the bright light."

老三按照仙女的吩咐，
来到了两个海子的中间。
他等着吉祥与邪恶开战，
他等着恶魔从黑浪中出现。

突然一阵狂风骤起，
黑色的海子开始动荡。
海水随风越翻越急，
涌起了冲天的巨浪。

在黑浪怒吼的海心，
出现了骑黑马的大汉。
那就是凶狠恶毒的魔王，
他飞马扑向白色的海浪。

老三连忙张弓搭箭，
瞄准了魔王胸前的斑点。
黑马在黑浪上飞奔，
那闪亮的斑点在飞旋。

老三奋力一箭射去，
只听当啷一声巨响，
黑大汉一头栽下黑马，
滔天的黑浪飞快下降。

Following the directions of the fairies,

The third brother came to the place between the two lakes.

He waited for the fight between the auspicious spirit and the evil spirit;

He waited for the Demon from the black waves.

A gale started suddenly,

And the waves began to rise in the black lake.

With a wind the water soared higher and higher,

And became the towering waves.

In the midst of the black waves in the center of the lake,

A big black man appeared riding a black horse.

That was the fierce and evil Demon,

Who was riding his horse and flying at the white waves.

The third brother pulled his bowstring, mounted an arrow,

And aimed at the spot on the demon's chest.

The black horse was running on the black waves,

And the bright spot was rotating quickly.

The third brother shot his arrow with all his might,

And then a huge "bang" was heard.

The black man dropped from the black horse,

And the sky-high waves descended quickly.

这时白海还在翻腾，

老三忙念如意吉祥，

白色的海浪马上下降，

茫茫大地一片宁静安详。

At that time the white lake was still churning.

The third brother quickly recited the auspicious spells.

The white waves immediately began to descend,

And gradually the vast land became quiet and serene.

英雄选亲

The Hero Choosing His Bride

老三帮助了吉祥的白海，
老三射死了黑色的魔王。
老三背起神奇的弓箭，
老三胜利地离开了战场。

勇杀魔王的老三，
脚步匆匆翻过了山梁。
迎接凯旋的英雄，
三位仙女来到半路上。

"我们天天和魔王打仗，
一直未把魔王杀伤。
今天你消灭了邪恶的根源，
天下从此就安宁吉祥。

"你是天下最勇敢的英雄，
你帮我们实现了愿望。
为了感激你的恩情，
我们姐妹任你挑选。

"你选中了任何一个，
都愿做你的新娘。
和你在大地上成亲，

The third brother helped the auspicious white lake,

And shot the black Demon to death.

The third brother put the magic bow on his back,

And left the battle field in victory.

The third brother, who killed the Demon,

Climbed and crossed the ridges.

To meet the victorious hero,

The three fairies came to meet him half way.

"We fought against the Demon every day,

But could not kill the Demon.

Today you have wiped out the root of evil.

The world will be peaceful and auspicious from now on."

"You are the bravest hero in the world;

You have helped us to realize our wish.

In order to thank you for your help,

You can choose one of us for your bride.

"You can choose anyone of us,

And she will be willing to be your bride.

She will marry you on the land,

把人类重新繁衍。"

老三听了仙女的话，
高兴得脸红心慌。
姐妹三人全都好，
喜欢哪个费思量。

大姐见老三犯为难，
灵机一动把办法想：
"你去躲到山垭口，
等着我们来翻梁。

"我们姐妹化身来，
喜欢哪个准你点。
只要轻轻碰一下，
我们马上把身现。"

老三躲到垭口上，
等着仙女来翻梁。
手里拿着弓和箭，
等着要把爱人点。

一只老虎奔过来，
只听呼呼山风响。

And increase the number of people again. "

Hearing what the fairies said,
The third brother flushed and became panicked.
As all three sisters were excellent,
It was difficult to choose one from them.

The eldest sister sensed his dilemma,
And came up with an idea:
"You can go to the mountain pass,
And wait for us to go through. "

"We will come as animals,
And you can choose the one you like.
You only need to touch lightly,
And we will change into our original forms immediately."

The third brother hid at the mountain pass
To wait for the fairies to come.
He had his bow and arrows in his hand,
Waiting to touch the one he loved.

One tiger approached quickly,
And brought a whistling wind with it.

老三一见脚发软，
骇得跌坐在地上。

接着一只金钱豹，
几步纵到山梁上。
老三一见心发颤，
连忙闪身躲一旁。

随后草木倒两边，
呼呼蹿来一条蟒。
老三从来怕见蛇，
一见巨蟒淌冷汗。

大蟒刚要过山梁，
老三箭步纵上前。
三个仙女都过完，
再不动手没指望。

老三挥动手中弓，
刚好点着蟒尾尖。
大蟒原是三姑娘，
她马上摇身把形现。

"好个勇敢的小伙子，

The third brother's feet trembled and could not move;

He was frightened and dropped to the ground.

Then came a leopard,

Which jumped onto the ridge with a few leaps.

Seeing the coming leopard he began to tremble,

And instinctively he stepped aside.

Grass and trees being pushed aside,

A hissing python sprang out.

The third brother was always afraid of snakes;

Seeing the huge python he began to sweat.

The python was just going out of the mountain pass;

The third brother jumped forward.

Because all the fairies had gone through,

There was no one left if he did not move.

The third brother swished his bow,

Just to touch the tail of the python.

The python was actually the third sister;

In a flash she changed into her former self.

"You brave young man,

我看你实在瞎了眼。
两个姐姐你不碰，
选了小妹不体面。

"我家大姐最能干，
只用一棵青稞面，
能做九个大粑粑，
为何不把大姐选？

"我家二姐也能干，
只用一棵青稞面，
能做六个大粑粑，
为何不把二姐选？

"唯有小妹没出息，
我用一棵青稞面，
只做三个大粑粑，
为何要把小妹选？"

三妹越骂他越喜，
老三心里像蜜甜。
老三拉着三妹说：
"我俩天生有良缘。

I think you are really stupid.

You did not touch my two elder sisters;

It is not decent for you to choose me."

"My eldest sister is the most capable.

With the flour of a grain of barley,

She can make nine big griddle cakes.

Why didn't you choose my eldest sister?"

"My second sister is also very capable.

With the flour of a grain of barley,

She can make six big griddle cakes.

Why didn't you choose my second sister?"

"I myself am the least capable.

With the flour of a grain of barley,

I can only make three big griddle cakes.

Why do you choose me?"

The more she criticized him, the happier he was,

In his heart the third brother felt sweet.

He caught the hand of the third sister and said,

"We two have destined to be married."

"大姐二姐本事大，
美丽的三妹也不差。
只用一棵青稞面，
能做三个大粑粑。

"你我每人吃一个，
一个粑粑还剩下。
等我两个成亲后，
那个粑粑喂娃娃。"

三妹听了羞答答，
拉着老三说悄悄话：
"既然你爱我是真心，
我就下凡把你嫁。

"只是我们三姐妹，
父王亲命离天庭，
前来大地上杀妖魔，
前来大地上布吉祥。

"如今魔王已除掉，
你帮我们打了胜仗。
要回天庭报父王，
父王恩准再下凡。"

"The two elder sisters are very capable,

But you beautiful third sister are not bad either.

With the flour of a grain of barley,

You can make three big griddle cakes."

"Each of us can have one;

There is still one left.

After we get married,

The remaining one is to feed the baby."

The third sister was shy;

She held his hand and whispered,

"Now that you really love me,

I shall come to the land to marry you."

"But we three sisters,

Left heaven with father god's order,

To come to the ground to kill devils,

And spread peace on the land.

"Now that the Demon has been killed,

Because you helped us to win victory.

We have to go back to heaven to report to father god,

And then come back with his permission."

三个仙女齐展飞，
带着老三飞天庭。
要向天神去报喜，
要向天神去求婚。

天庭一派金碧辉煌，
老三简直睁不开眼睛。
四人来到天神大殿，
跪向父王呈报详情。

大姐说邪恶已经除掉，
妖魔鬼怪已经杀尽，
吉祥弥漫着茫茫大地，
大地上万物一片安宁。

二姐说洪水过后的地上，
只剩一个孤独的男人，
他是一位勇敢的英雄，
他用神箭帮助了我们。

三妹说为了报答深恩，
她已答应和英雄成亲，
恳请父王恩准女儿，

The three girls began to fly to heaven,

Bringing the third brother with them.

They would bring good news to the god,

And ask for permission from the god.

The heaven was grand and golden;

The third brother could hardly open his eyes.

They came to the god's hall,

Knelt to report to father god.

The eldest sister said that evils had been wiped out;

The Demon and devils had been killed;

Fortune and good luck filled the world;

Everything on the earth was in peace.

The second sister said that on the land after the flood,

Only one lonely man survived.

He was a brave hero,

Who used his arrows to help us.

The third sister said that to repay his kindness,

She had promised to marry him.

She requested permission from father god,

让她下凡去发展人类。

高贵的木多丁巴天神，
不想让女儿嫁给凡人。
他要考验小伙子是否能干，
他要考验小伙子是否真诚。

To permit her to go down to the earth to live with the young man.

The noble God Muduodingba,

Did not want his daughter to marry a mortal.

He wanted to test if the young man was capable;

He wanted to test if the young man was honest.

天神的考验
God's Tests

到了第二天早上，
天神一副笑脸盈盈。
他交给老三一把砍刀，
叫老三去砍一片森林。

老三砍了三天三夜，
只砍倒了大树几根。
那一片黑森森的老林，
老三一辈子也砍不尽。

小伙子丧失了信心，
他去找三妹诉苦情。
那片老林他砍不完，
他只好孤独地回凡尘。

三妹笑着告诉他，
克服困难要有耐心。
叫他第二天再去砍，
叫他把方法记分明。

"九把斧头放九方，
说声'神斧帮我砍'，
斧头自己会砍树，

The next morning,

The god showed a smiling appearance.

He gave the third brother a cutting knife,

And told him to cut a forest.

The third brother cut for three days and three nights,

But he only cut down a few big trees.

The big bushy forest,

Would take him more than his whole life to cut down.

The young man lost his confidence,

And went to complain to the third sister.

As he could not cut down the forest,

He could only go back to the mortal world alone.

The smiling third sister told him that

He needed patience to overcome difficulties.

She told him to cut again the next day;

She told him to remember some tips.

"Put nine axes in nine directions,

And say 'magic axes, please help me to cut'.

The axes will cut by themselves;

你可抱手歇一旁。"

老三按照三妹的话，
带了九把斧头上山林。
只一天老林全砍光，
一把大火烧成灰。

小伙子来复天神命，
天神夸他有本领。
叫他再去开生荒，
撒下荞种看收成。

小伙子开了三天荒，
一双手掌血淋淋。
九架梁子十架坡，
他一辈子也挖不尽。

好心的三妹又助他：
"九把锄头放九方，
说声'神锄帮我挖'，
你只消一旁躲阴凉。"

九架梁子十架山，
老三一天全挖翻。

You can just rest beside the forest."

Following the third sister's direction,
The third brother brought nine axes to the forest.
It took him only one day to cut all trees down.
Then he set a fire to burn all the trees to ash.

The young man came to report to the god,
Who praised his ability.
Then the god asked him to reclaim the virgin land,
And sow buckwheat seeds and wait for the harvest.

The young man worked for three days.
His palms were full of blisters and calluses.
To cultivate land on the nine ridges and the ten slopes,
He could not finish the task in his whole life.

The kindhearted third sister helped him again,
"Lay nine hoes in nine different directions,
And say 'magic hoes, please dig the land for me'.
You only need to rest beside the land."

Cultivating nine ridges and ten slopes
Took the young man only one day.

开好荒地要播种，
天神故意来刁难。

天神只给三抔种，
三抔荞种撒九山。
待到秋来收荞子，
九十只桶要装满。

到了荞熟收割时，
九十只木桶装不满。
天神追问小伙子，
别的荞子去哪方？

老三心慌无主张，
推说老牛偷吃光。
天神叫人破牛肚，
一颗荞子也不见。

织布的三妹说了话：
老牛被杀太冤枉。
荞子是被鸽子吃，
谁吃该由谁来还。

老三听了更发慌，

After the land was reclaimed, it was time to sow seeds.

The god made it difficult on purpose.

The god gave him only three handfuls of seeds,

To be sown on nine mountains.

By the time of harvesting the buckwheat in autumn,

Ninety barrels had to be full with buckwheat.

By the time of harvesting the buckwheat,

Not all ninety barrels were filled.

The god inquired of the young man,

Where was the other buckwheat?

The third brother was in a panic and had no idea.

He said the other buckwheat had been eaten by the ox.

The god demanded to cut open the stomach of the ox,

But no buckwheat was found.

The third sister, who was weaving, said:

The ox was wrongly killed.

The buckwheat was eaten by pigeons;

The one who ate the buckwheat should repay the buckwheat.

The third brother became more panicked.

鸽子难道比牛大？
九十只鸽子全吃饱，
那多荞子也无法还。

一只鸽子空中飞，
三妹取梭抛上天。
急飞的鸽子被打中，
扑扑棱棱落庭院。

破开鸽肚取荞子，
越取越多取不完。
鸽子肚子实在大，
九十只木桶全装满。

几次刁难都失败，
天神便起黑心肠。
他要老三挤虎奶，
想叫老三死虎山。

第一天挤回狼奶来，
第二天挤回豹奶来。
牛马不惊狗不跳，
天神知是假虎奶。

Was it possible that a pigeon was bigger than an ox?

Even if ninety pigeons ate to their full,

They could not repay the buckwheat.

One pigeon was flying in the sky at that time.

The third sister threw her shuttle into the sky.

The flying pigeon was hit by the shuttle;

It flapped its wings and landed in the courtyard.

The stomach of the pigeon was cut open for buckwheat;

Endless buckwheat was taken out.

The stomach of the pigeon was really big;

Ninety wooden barrels were filled with the buckwheat.

Seeing all his tricks failed,

The god had another bad idea.

He demanded the third brother to milk a tiger,

Wishing the young man to die on the mountain.

On the first day wolf milk was brought back;

On the second day leopard milk was brought back;

Because oxen, horses and dogs were not scared,

The god knew that it was not tiger's milk.

不取虎奶亲不成，
要取虎奶太凶险。
眼看小伙子要遭难，
聪明的三妹又相帮：

"三天三夜大雪后，
母老虎去阳山烤太阳，
虎崽却在阴山面，
躲在洞里把身藏。

"那时你去杀虎崽，
剥下虎皮穿身上。
等到母虎回洞来，
装着吃奶去挤奶。

"趁着母虎往上跳，
你就挤奶莫慌张。
只要用手挤三下，
你快出洞把身返。"

老三挤回虎奶来，
牛马发抖猪翻圈。
天神实在无话说，
只好让女儿下凡间。

Without tiger milk the marriage was impossible,

But it was too difficult to milk a tiger.

Seeing that the young man would lose his life,

The clever third sister once again offered a good idea:

"After three days and three nights' snow,

The tigress will go to a sunny mountain for sunshine.

The tiger cubs will hide in the cave,

On the shady side of the mountain."

"At that time you can go to kill one tiger cub;

Skin the cub and put on its fur.

When the tigress comes back,

Pretend to be the cub and get the milk."

"When the tigress jumps upward,

You can squeeze the breast and get the milk.

You only need to squeeze three times,

And then come out of the cave and come back."

When the third brother brought back the tiger's milk,

The oxen and horses trembled and the pigs jumped out of their cages.

The god had nothing to say;

He had to allow his daughter to go to the mortal world.

种子的由来
The Origin of Seeds

仙女跟小伙子到了地上，
恩恩爱爱地把家安。
他们边吃着天上的食物，
边辛勤地挖地开荒。

荒地开了一块又一块，
可没有一颗种子撒上。
圈房修了一座又一座，
可没有一个牲口关上。

三姑娘决定回娘家要种，
有了种子日子才能长远。
临走时三姑娘依依不舍，
捏个灰姑娘拿给老三：

"她会为你做家务，
她可以陪你做伙伴。
可你一定要记住，
不能接近她的身旁。"

天上一天地上三年，
三姑娘要种去上天，
在娘家才住了四天，

The angel and the young man came to the earth;

They settled down lovingly.

They ate the food brought from heaven;

Industriously they cultivated and reclaimed the land.

The land was reclaimed one piece after another,

But they did not have any seeds for the land.

Stables were built one after another,

But they did not have any cattle for the stables.

The third sister decided to go home to beg for seeds,

Because life would not last long without seeds.

The third sister was reluctant to leave;

She molded a girl out of ashes for the third brother.

"She will do housework for you,

And she will serve as your peer.

But you must remember that,

You must not have physical contact with her."

One day in heaven was three years on the ground.

The third sister went to heaven for seeds,

And stayed at her home for four days,

地上已过了十二年。

老三久等不见仙女回来，
便接近了家中的灰姑娘。
和灰姑娘生了孩子，
渐渐把三仙女遗忘。

三姑娘要了五谷种子，
三姑娘要了猪马牛羊。
她捧着吉祥的海螺花，
告别了天庭驾云下凡。

三姑娘来到房屋上空，
见有孩子在院里耍玩，
知道丈夫爱了灰姑娘，
三妹一气要返回天上。

这时老三正在犁地，
突然看见久别的新娘，
见她要把种子带回天上
连忙去取来了弓箭。

三妹正带着种子升天，
老三朝她射开了箭。

Which equalled twelve years on the ground.

The third brother waited for a long time but did not see her return;

He had physical contact with the ash girl at home.

They had children,

And gradually he forgot the angel.

The third sister brought all kinds of grain seeds,

And pigs, horses, cattle and sheep.

She had some auspicious conch flowers in her hand,

Bid farewell to heaven and flew to the mortal world by a cloud.

When she flew to the sky over the house,

She saw children playing in the courtyard.

Realizing that her husband had fallen in love with the ash girl,

In anger she wanted to go back to heaven.

The third brother was ploughing the field,

When he suddenly saw his long-separated wife.

Seeing that she was taking seeds back to heaven,

He rushed to fetch his bow and arrows.

While the third sister was bringing seeds back to heaven,

The third brother shot his arrows at her bags.

随着一声声箭响，
种子纷纷掉落地面。

骡马的蹄子凹进去，
牛羊的蹄子成两半，
鸡狗的脚板成爪子，
就是那次被箭射伤。

五谷种子射下来，
落地生根就长粮。
三妹见了越发恨，
飞到地上来猛抢。

原来的麦子苗棵高，
麦粒从根结到梢尖。
三姑娘往上抹一把，
只剩几颗颗在梢尖。

原来的苞谷更是宝，
苞谷秆儿是甘蔗，
头顶的天花是谷子，
每道结巴处都背包。

三妹将谷穗全抹掉，

With one arrow after another being shot,
All kinds of seeds fell to the ground.

Mules and horses' hoofs are concave;
Cattle and sheep's hoofs are split;
Chicken's feet and dogs' paws in present form,
They were caused by the injury of the arrow shots.

When all kinds of seeds fell to the ground,
They immediately took root and produced grains.
The third sister became angrier,
And flew to the ground to grab the grains.

The wheat had higher straw,
Which bore grains from roots to straw tips.
When the third sister grabbed upward,
Only a few grains were left at the top.

The maize was much better,
Their stalks being sweet canes,
The flowers at the top were rice;
At every knot there was an ear of maize.

The third sister grabbed away all the rice;

三妹将苞谷全扳光。
现在的苞谷背一包，
是三妹太急收漏掉。

三妹又接着收花荞，
划破了手掌鲜血淌。
殷红的血水染荞秆，
至今荞秆上留血斑。

三妹手痛大声骂：
"我要让甜荞变苦荞；
蔓菁煮了变成水，
背在背上压断腰！"

三妹愤恨变心的丈夫，
要把庄稼收回天上。
可终于没有全部收完，
留下了一些种子在地上。

大地上留下的庄稼，
全成了三妹咒的模样。
庄稼虽不如仙人的好了，
人类却靠它得到了发展。

The third sister pulled all the maize ears.

Now there is only one ear on each plant,

Because it is left by the hasty third sister.

The third sister went on to collect buckwheat.

Her hand was cut by the stalks and began to bleed.

Her blood stained the stalks of buckwheat,

And there is still the trace of blood on buckwheat stalks today.

The third sister felt the pain and began to curse:

"I will change sweet buckwheat into bitter buckwheat;

Turnip becomes water after being boiled,

And it's so heavy that it may break your back!"

As the third sister was angry at her husband's changed heart,

She wanted to bring all the crops back to heaven.

But she left some of them,

which were left on the earth and became seeds.

Though some crops were left on the ground,

They all changed into their present forms as the angel cursed.

Though the crops were not as good as the immortals',

Human beings developed because of them.

About the Translator

Liu Dezhou is a professor of English in the School of Foreign Languages and Literature at Yunnan Normal University. His recent publications include two monographs, *Studies and Practice of Reflexology* and *A Contrastive Study of Tautology in English and Chinese* and several articles in academic journals. He also participated in the translation or editing of several books and textbooks. Professor Liu is an experienced simultaneous interpreter and he has interpreted in over 200 international forums, workshops and seminars for many international organizations and Chinese ministries, departments and organizations in his spare time.

语文

九年级 下册

教
科
书

语文

又系温儒敏教授担任总主编。

王宁、张联荣、柳士镇、方智范、谭邦和、梁捷、郑桂华、陈双新、王岱等审查专家提出了很多宝贵的修改意见，对教科书的修改完善给予了悉心指导和倾力帮助。在教育部的组织下，广大一线优秀教师反馈了很多意见和建议，保证了教学的适切性。在试教试用过程中，我们得到了重庆市，江苏省，湖南省，陕西省等省（市）教育科学研究院（所），教研室及一线教师的大力支持，他们的意见和建议为教科书的进一步完善提供了保障。

人民教育出版社承担了教科书的编辑出版工作。在组织编写，试教试用等方面给予了全方位的协助。人民教育出版社中语室全体同仁始终是教科书编写的中坚力量。感谢吕敬人等为本套教科书的整体设计提供了艺术指导，感谢丁永康为本套教科书"读读写写"栏目书写了硬笔书法范字。此外，对教科书的编写、出版提供过帮助的同仁和社会各界朋友还有很多，在此一并表示诚挚的谢意。

期盼使用本套教科书的广大师生、家长提出宝贵意见，我们将集思广益，不断修订，使教科书趋于完善。

编者

2018年12月

联系方式

电　话：010-58758959

电子邮箱：jcfk@pep.com.cn